Ten escorted her to the dance floor and pulled her into his arms. He knew this was a mistake.

She pressed her body close and they began moving in sync. He forgot she was off-limits, that this was a ruse to get a rise out of her now ex-husband. When she relaxed and laid her head on his chest, he closed his eyes and willed himself not to physically react to the smell of her hair and the feel of her skin. The dress she was wearing left her arms and part of her back bare and her skin was silky and warm. She smelled of honeysuckle, fresh. He breathed her in.

Lana's body trembled slightly. Was there any turning back from this? Their first dance on her dad's deck had been nothing like this. It felt like a prelude to lovemaking and not just lovemaking but hot, uncontrollable, mind-blowing sex.

She tilted her head up and as soon as she met his eyes, she knew: He felt it, too.

He wanted her, wanted her as much as she wanted him. She took a deep breath and let it out. "We're in trouble, aren't we?"

JANICE SIMS

is the author of twenty-one novels and has had stories included in nine anthologies. She is the recipient of an Emma Award for her novel *Desert Heat* and two Romance in Color awards: an Award of Excellence for her novel *For Keeps* and a Best Novella award for her short story in the anthology *A Very Special Love*. She has been nominated for a Career Achievement Award by *RT Book Reviews* and her novel *Temptation's Song* was nominated for Best Kimani Romance Series in 2010 by *RT Book Reviews*. A longtime member of Romance Writers of America, she lives in Central Florida with her family.

Escape
WITH
ME

JANICE SIMS

HARLEQUIN® KIMANI™ ROMANCE

Recycling programs
for this product may
not exist in your area.

ISBN-13: 978-0-373-86302-0

ESCAPE WITH ME

Copyright © by Janice Sims

For questions and comments about the quality of this book, please contact us
at CustomerService@Harlequin.com.

Printed in U.S.A.

H HARLEQUIN®
™ www.Harlequin.com

Dear Reader,

How well do you know your significant other? I've been married for a lot of years, but just the other day my husband said something that made me rethink how well I really know him. Luckily, in most relationships, the secrets each partner keeps are not the sinister kind. In this story, however, Lana Corday is devastated by her husband's secrets. Will she allow his behavior to derail her life? Or will she pull herself together and maybe even get a little payback in the process?

If, after reading *Escape with Me,* you'd like to send me a message you can email me at Jani569432@aol.com or visit my website, www.janicesims.com. I'm also on Facebook.

For those of you who're not yet online, you can write me at Post Office Box 811, Mascotte, FL 34753-0811.

All the best,

Janice Sims

Thanks, again, to Shannon Criss, whose editorial assistance was very much appreciated. Also thanks to all the lovely people of the Outer Banks who were so friendly and didn't mind answering my many questions about their home!

Chapter 1

"Do you want your life back?" Grant Robinson asked Lana Corday as he stared intensely into her big brown eyes. Lana swallowed hard and lowered her gaze.

Grant, impeccably dressed in a tailored suit, was her attorney and one of the few men she still trusted.

He sat behind his cherrywood desk while Lana, too restless to sit, stood. He observed her as she mentally wrestled with his question. She had a sprinkling of freckles across the bridge of her nose and wide-spaced eyes that made her face, if not classically beautiful, very appealing. Her nose was strong, which gave her character, and her full mouth with a plump lower lip made him wonder about her stamina in bed. An inappropriate thought, since he was her attorney. But he *was* also a man. She was five-nine, had mocha-colored skin, her eyes were a warm brown with gold striations in them, and she had chin-length burnt-auburn hair—a shade of which Grant had never seen on any other woman. Once he'd asked her where she'd gotten that shade of hair, she'd laughed and said her great-grandfather was Scottish.

Lana sighed and walked over to the huge picture window in Grant's San Francisco office.

She could see the Golden Gate Bridge from there. A few luxury yachts were in the Bay along with commercial cargo ships. San Francisco was her dream city. She adored the San Francisco Museum of Modern Art. Loved traipsing all over Fisherman's Wharf and often ending her visit with dinner at Alioto's. And she never tired of the luxury of the Palace Hotel. But now the city had lost its charm for her.

She turned back to face Grant. He was watching her with a quizzical expression on his handsome, tanned face. In a gesture of frustration he ran his hand through his thick, dark brown wavy hair that had begun to gray at the temples. Sighing, he asked, "Are you ever going to answer me? He abandoned you, Lana. It's time you admitted that."

"He was blown up on his boat. That's not abandonment, that's death," Lana said, still sticking to her assertion that Jeremy was deceased and not a criminal on the run as Grant and any number of other people, including the FBI, believed.

Looking out over the Bay again, her mind took her back to that fateful day nearly six months ago when Jeremy had kissed her goodbye and left for an outing on their yacht. "Just a few hours to clear my mind, babe," he had jauntily said before disappearing from her life forever.

Minutes later she was racing down to the dock next to the boathouse at their Bay-area home and looking in horror at what was left of the yacht, smoldering, listing leeward in the water. It had blown up with Jeremy aboard before it had even gotten fifty yards from the dock.

"There's no evidence Jeremy was onboard," Grant reminded her doggedly. "Believe me, if he had been killed aboard that yacht, forensics would have found at least some of his DNA. In two days he was going on trial for fraud, and if he lost his case he was going to be locked up for a very long time. He didn't want to go to prison so he blew up his own yacht and disappeared, hoping that desperate act would convince the authorities he was dead."

Lana stubbornly shook her head. She clasped the gold locket around her neck, a gift from Jeremy. "No, he loved me. He wouldn't have intentionally left me to face this on my own. He has to be dead."

Grant had seen this before, the loyalty of abandoned women who clung to any shred of hope where their worthless husbands were concerned. Although with Lana Corday, her husband had been worthless on a monumental scale. He'd allegedly bilked nearly half a billion dollars from investors who had trusted him with their hard-earned savings, many of them retirees hoping to make their golden years easier. Since Jeremy had "blown up" on his yacht, the authorities had successfully tracked down a small portion of the pilfered funds. The bulk of it was still missing, though.

As for Lana, she seemed to subsist on the belief that her husband was dead and that had been the only reason he was not around now facing the music and defending that he was not the villain the press had painted him to be.

By virtue of her connection with him, she was also being vilified. Before her husband's legal problems, Lana had been a successful interior designer. Now her client list was dwindling at an incredible rate. With Jeremy's assets frozen, she had to depend on what little savings she had prior to this whole mess. Plus, whatever she earned.

With clients abandoning her left and right, she could barely pay her bills anymore.

Grant gestured to the leather chair in front of his desk. "Sit down, Lana, and listen to me." He watched as she sat down, a lithe figure in a slim-fitting off-white sleeveless dress whose hem fell just above her well-shaped knees. Her style was classic yet casual.

She crossed her legs and hugged herself. Grant noticed that she'd lost weight since the last time he'd seen her. Tall and athletic, Lana had a healthy, fit body that she kept in shape by running, weight-lifting, and yoga. He feared that she'd started exercising at the detriment of her health: running away from her problems. Her arms, formerly well-formed and muscled but feminine, were now looking a bit masculine. His biceps weren't even that defined and he worked out nearly every day.

He continued in a gentle voice. "I've drawn up divorce papers for you to sign, Lana. I'm your friend. Have been since we met more than five years ago; before you met Jeremy, I might add. I wouldn't suggest you do this unless I was sure it's the way out of your financial problems. In the state of California you are within your rights to divorce a husband on grounds of abandonment."

"I didn't ask you to draw up divorce papers!" Lana cried, clearly upset by the notion. Her brilliant brown eyes sparked angry fire at him.

"Now, hear me out," Grant pleaded. "Divorcing Jeremy would send a message to everyone concerned that you're separating yourself from him and everything he's accused of. Let's be practical, Lana. The house and everything else of value has been seized by the government. You're living in a one-room apartment. You have very few clients anymore. You can't live on air. Sure, you were doing very well before you met him and you could do well without him once again, if only your association with him didn't taint you, but it does! You have to send a clear message that you're washing your hands of him so that you can reclaim your life."

Lana stood up suddenly. Tears sat in her eyes. "I'll have to think about it," she said with finality.

"You do that," said Grant, keeping his tone soft so as not to upset her further. "But I've got one more thing to say. Stop punishing yourself. You've lost weight, chopped off your hair and I suspect you're also over-doing the running, am I right?"

He waited, his eyes remaining on her stricken face. He knew he'd struck a nerve.

"It's the only thing that gets me tired enough to sleep," she mumbled in her defense. "I'm trying not to resort to pills."

"Kudos on that," Grant said. "I don't want you going anywhere near pills. But I do want you to take a good look at yourself in the mirror when you get home and ask yourself why you're putting yourself through hell over a man who never deserved you in the first place. You come from a lineage of tough North Carolinians. I remember you telling me about your great-grandfather who was a rescue-station commander in the Outer Banks in the late 1800s, and how your father, Aaron, rescued a family after their boat sank off shore near his Pea Island home. How would he react if he saw you right now?"

He could see the horror at that prospect mirrored in her eyes. He laughed softly.

"Have you even told your father what you're going through?"

"I gave him the basics," Lana allowed. She took a deep breath. "He told me to come home."

"Why don't you?"

"Because I can take care of myself," she said, as if that were explanation enough. Then, as though their conversation were over, she added, "Thanks, Grant. I've got to be going."

She hurriedly pulled on her jacket. The March morning air was a bit chilly in the city.

"Don't wait too long to make a decision about the divorce," Grant warned. "You could go visit your dad for a few months and come back a free woman and ready to start your life over."

Lana found herself laughing softly at Grant's ludicrous suggestion as she hurried to the bank of elevators in the elegant building in which Grant had his offices. The building boasted plenty of glass and steel, the former allowing in lots of sunshine to brighten up the modern interior of marble floors, sparse, ultra-modern furnishings and colorful paintings on the walls by local artists, a breed that in Lana's opinion, San Francisco never seemed to run out of.

She continued to laugh. Grant was such an optimist. If only it were that easy to start over again. But, how do you go on when the love of your life turns out to be a criminal? It might have appeared that she was the long-suffering widow, but her father had not raised a fool. She knew a little about boats, having been raised on them by a fisherman father. She had known that yacht like the back of her hand. She knew how to pilot it. She had been the one to teach Jeremy. There was no way that boat could blow up without being sabotaged. She had had it inspected less than a month before the incident. Jeremy, of course, had not known that. He left such things to her. The boat mechanic had gone down his semi-annual checklist. The fire inspector had said the explosion had been caused by a faulty fuel system. There was a leak and upon ignition, a spark had lit the fuel thereby causing the yacht to explode. But the boat mechanic was a man Lana had trusted the past four years to do a thorough job of maintaining the yacht. He had checked for leaks, corrosion, and crack-free hoses— even if there was adequate slackness to account for any vibration that could cause the hoses to wriggle loose. Of course the mechanic had been interviewed by the police and had sworn that he had given the yacht a complete inspection and had found nothing at all wrong with the fuel system.

Lana suspected the fuel system had been tampered with. And the only person who could have done it was Jeremy. The question was why? That had been the first instance in which her faith in her husband had been shaken. Since then, in retrospect, she realized that a lot of things Jeremy had done had been suspicious.

She laughed again, and this time she wasn't alone. The man in the elevator with her laughed nervously along with her. She supposed he thought it was best to humor an insane person.

Lana looked at him and said, "Sorry, something just struck me as funny and I had to laugh." *To keep from crying,* she thought.

Why had Jeremy faked his death? Because he was guilty of the charges leveled against him, that's why. He was a slimy con artist. If she hadn't been so blindly in love she would have spotted the characteristics that were so apparent to her now. He could charm anyone. It didn't matter if the victim was male or female. Inside of two minutes he would have you eating out of his hand. But while he could extract every little secret out of you, and appeared to be pouring his heart out to you, he actually revealed very little about himself. He said he was an orphan who grew up in the system so there were no relatives who could corroborate his claims. Another one of his lies, as it turned out.

On the street, Lana walked with purpose. She was scheduled to meet a potential client at a coffeehouse only a few blocks from here. Over the phone, Gia Burrows had sounded enthusiastic and honestly impressed with Lana's past projects in and around the city. Gia said she was a friend of a long-time client of Lana's and said that client had suggested she meet Lana. Curiously, she had not told Lana the name of the person who had referred her.

Minutes later, she was standing in front of the trendy coffeehouse. Suddenly nervous, she smoothed her dress down in an attempt to hide the fact that she was wiping her sweaty palms. Taking a deep breath, she entered the establishment and her eyes scanned the place. Young professionals, mostly, populated the tables and booths. The delightful smell of fresh-roasted coffee assailed her nostrils and relaxed her. She could use a cup of java.

A petite brunette wearing designer jeans and a sleeveless silk top in jade stood up and waved her over. "Lana?" she called.

Smiling, Lana crossed the room and shook hands with the woman who appeared to be in her early thirties. Sitting down, Lana said, "Hello, Gia, nice to meet you"

Gia smiled. "Thanks for meeting me. I'm at my wit's end trying to get our place done before July. Derek's parents are supposed to come for a month-long visit and his mother hates me, totally hates me. The last time she visited all she did was complain about the amateurish way I'd decorated the house." She lowered her voice conspiratorially. "Her family owned a mansion on Nob Hill. She and my father-in-law live in Montecito now. By comparison, I come from the ranch-house set. She never lets me forget how lucky I am to have landed Derek."

Lana's first impression was that she liked Gia Burrows. However, lately, due to what she'd gone through with Jeremy, she reserved judgment.

"I feel for you," she told Gia with a smile. "But if you don't mind me asking before we go any further, who was it that referred you to me?"

Gia was one of those people who turned red when she was embarrassed. That was the first clue that something was wrong here.

She cleared her throat. "Well, actually, I…um…read about you online." She smiled, showing perfect white teeth. Looking sheepish, she continued, "I thought it would totally piss my mother-in-law off when she found out who decorated the house. She and my father-in-law had invested money with your *late* husband."

Lana was speechless with shock after hearing that. However, somewhere in the back of her mind she was thinking she really shouldn't be surprised that the only reason someone was thinking of hiring her was to piss someone else off. She was also disgusted with herself because she was seriously thinking of accepting the assignment. After all, she had bills to pay.

The part of her that still had some pride wouldn't bend to the desperate Lana in her, though.

She got up. As she looked down at Gia Burrows who was still sitting, she said, "Look, I'm not judging you on how you get your jollies. Several of my clients have just picked me out the phone book, but the reason you chose me makes me leery. So, I'll have to say no thanks."

Gia looked genuinely let down by her decision. Pouting, she said, "Are you sure? I'd pay you anything you asked for. If you met my mother-in-law, I assure you that you'd totally be on my side."

"Look, Gia, if you should change your mind and

you seriously want to work with me and it's not just to stick it to your mother-in-law, then you know how to reach me. You say you have read about me online. Then you know my life is pretty screwed up right now. I'm barely keeping my head above water and I don't have time for frivolous offers of work. I need concrete business opportunities."

With that, Lana left the coffeehouse.

She heard Gia mutter, "Damn!" as she walked away.

Lana had already quickly walked three blocks back in the direction of Grant's office building. Her encounter with Gia *had* helped her make up her mind about the divorce. Jeremy was most likely somewhere getting on with his life. It was time she got on with hers.

She took out her cell phone and dialed Grant's cell phone.

"Hey, Lana," he answered in his usual upbeat manner.

"Are you busy right now?"

"Yes, but I can see you in half an hour," he replied.

"Great. I'm coming to sign those papers."

"All right," he answered cheerfully. "See you soon."

She then hung up the phone. *Damn you, Jeremy, for putting me in this position. You'd* better *run. Run far away. Because if I ever get my hands on you again, you're going to be in for a world of pain.*

As Lana shoved her phone into its slot in her purse,

she heard heavy breathing behind her. She turned to see Gia Burrows hurrying toward her.

"Lana, wait. You're right. I wanted to hire you for all the wrong reasons." Gia stopped in front of her and took a moment to catch her breath. "I apologize, but I really need you. I know you're one of the best and if you'll forgive me for my crassness I'm ready to make you a serious offer."

Lana smiled at her. Was she going to turn down a genuine offer of employment? No way. She stuck out her hand for Gia to shake. "Apology accepted."

Chapter 2

Tennison Isles made it a habit of taking the stairs. His work schedule made it difficult to get to the gym every day. However, as a special agent with the FBI he had to stay in good physical condition. As he stepped onto the thirteenth floor from the stairwell this morning, he had nearly collided with the special-agent-in-charge, Josh Kagen.

Kagen was in his mid-forties, of average height, and stocky with thick brown hair that he wore so close to his scalp from a distance he looked bald. Ten was thirty-five years old, six foot four, weighed 225 and his body was honed not just from walking up stairs but running, weight-lifting and twenty years of martial arts.

"Ten, you're just the guy I wanted to see. I suppose you heard about that Corday investor who tried to commit suicide. If his wife hadn't come home in the nick of time, he would have done himself in using a 1965 Mustang. He'd passed out, and she got there in just enough time to turn off the ignition and open the garage door."

Ten was about to say that he'd heard the report on the morning news. The deputy director often asked rhetorical questions, especially when he felt strongly about a case, as he did about the Jeremy Corday case.

Kagen began walking toward his office. Ten fell into step beside him.

"I feel for the family," Ten said, "And the widow. I'm sure she was glad the hoopla had died down a bit. Now the media will be clamoring for her thoughts on the matter."

Those who worked the case had started referring to Lana Corday as the widow even though they didn't believe Jeremy Corday was dead.

"How is he?" Ten inquired about the man who had attempted suicide. He was certain Kagen, known for his thoroughness, had gotten an update on the man's condition.

"He's going to be fine," said Kagen as he opened the door to his office and entered the large utilitarian furnished space. It complemented its owner, as it was highly efficient.

Kagen did not sit down but paced the room as he

continued, "I don't know about you, Ten, but I'm feeling mighty frustrated with the lack of progress we've had finding Corday. There's no paper trail, no sighting of him on airport security cameras, absolutely nothing! People are suffering because of him. Losing their homes, senior citizens have had to go out and find work to make ends meet in this economy." He punched the air with clenched fists. "I *know* he's got that money stashed in a bank in the States, possibly right here in San Francisco. But if his wife is somehow hiding something or is the key to the location of those funds, we haven't been able to connect her."

Ten had headed the team that had had Lana Corday under surveillance for the past seven months. He knew her personal life inside and out. What time she left her apartment in the morning, how often she ran, whom she saw during the day, and which jobs she was currently working on. If Jeremy Corday had tried to contact her, Ten would have known. Her phone records were devoid of anything out of the ordinary. No calls from a fugitive husband.

"Maybe he's truly dead," Ten ventured. He didn't really believe it, but was being the devil's advocate just for the sake of argument.

"He's too slippery to be dead," Kagen quickly stated. Scowling, he faced Ten. "There's got to be a way to smoke that rat out of his hidey-hole."

Ten had been giving that particular challenge some thought. Before he could reason with himself or talk himself out of speaking up at the risk of his idea sounding far-fetched and subsequently being shot down by Kagen, he cleared his throat and said, "I really don't think Corday is going to show his face in San Francisco. There's too much of a chance of his being spotted. But, if we could get the widow in a more remote location, say maybe, the Outer Banks, where Lana's father lives, your rat might nibble on the bait."

"But how do you propose we accomplish that, short of going to her and asking her to help us entrap her husband? I doubt she'd go for that even if she had no clue as to his business dealings and it's beginning to dawn on her what kind of man she married."

"No, but maybe her father isn't such a big fan of Corday's," Ten suggested.

Interested, as the spark in his gray eyes proved, Kagen said, "Go on."

"I can go to Mr. Braithwaite and explain our predicament, emphasizing the fact that his daughter could very well be in danger. What if she's in possession of something Corday needs in order to access the rest of the money? I believe her when she says he never gave her a safe-deposit key or any other important item for safe keeping. That doesn't mean he didn't hide something in her personal possessions that she's unaware of. She needs our protection. A father might respond to that."

Kagen smiled. "You have my permission to give it a shot."

* * *

"Lana, Lana! A word, please?"

It was dusk, and Lana had just returned home after a long day of putting the finishing touches on the Burrows house in the Russian Hill area. Reporter Gary Randall from the local ABC affiliate was very familiar to her. He was lean, had the polished good looks of an All-American athlete and was relentless when chasing down a story.

Although she wanted nothing more than to get inside her apartment, take off her shoes and relax, she turned to him with a resigned sigh, thinking that it was best to just get it over with. She already knew why he was here.

Luckily, the three-story Victorian home on Lombard Street where she had a one-room apartment was deserted this time of day. Her landlady didn't get home from her nursing job until after nine. The news van had drawn several curious neighbors to their windows for a look-see, though. A few were coming outside to get a better view.

Randall stood close to her as he began his questioning. "Lana, are you aware that one of your husband's victims tried to commit suicide?"

He didn't wait for her to comment before continuing with his line of questioning. "How do you feel about that? Do you feel guilty or sorry that the family suffered a near-tragedy? Or do you feel removed from it all? As if you bear no blame because, as you maintain, you knew nothing of your husband's fraudulent behavior?"

Lana looked straight into the camera. "I was very relieved to hear that Mrs. Carter got home in time to save her husband's life. I wish him a speedy recovery. And I hope the authorities will soon track down the funds that were taken from so many honest, hardworking people." She smiled warmly, after which she turned and went inside.

Gary Randall continued calling questions to her retreating back. When she firmly closed the door in his face he turned back around and said into the camera, "As you can see, Lana Corday remains one cool customer, showing no emotions whatsoever in the face of this horrible, horrible development in her husband's ongoing case."

"What a prick!" Gia said upon seeing the report the next day at noon while she and Lana were in the beautifully decorated kitchen of her home. It was her new favorite room in the house. Lana had turned what was once a cold, austere place into a warm, inviting room that was now deservedly the center of the home. She loved the rich earth tones of the tile on the floor and the cabinets and the deep red of the backsplash. There were two islands, one for food preparation, the other for family and guests to gather around to eat the meals Gia and her husband would cook. They were both budding chefs who loved feeding friends and family.

Lana looked across one of the islands into the face
of the woman she had come to consider a friend. During the three months it had taken her to redecorate
Gia's home, they had shared confidences. Lana had
told her she suspected Jeremy was still alive and was
guilty of the charges leveled against him. Gia had told
Lana that at first Derek had married her to spite his
overprotective rich parents, but they had fallen in love
and now they were devoted to each other. So much
so that Derek had given his blessings when she'd told
him she wanted to hire Lana to decorate their home.
Gia had to promise Derek not to gloat about it to her
mother-in-law. That admittedly took some fun out of
it for Gia, but she agreed to her husband's terms. Now
she and Lana were sitting on high stools enjoying cups
of Colombian coffee. Lana's eyes were on the TV. Gary
Randall had just made that comment about her being a
cool customer. Yet, Lana Corday was anything but the
emotionless character that Gary Randall was trying to
convince everyone she was. Lana fought back tears.

Gia got up and turned the TV off. "Enough of that,"
she said with a grin. She spun around on her designer
heels. "It's time to pay up for the fantastic job you did.
And I haven't forgotten I promised you anything you
asked for. So…" She whipped out her checkbook and
stood with a pen poised over it.

Lana laughed. "Please, Gia, there is already one too
many con artists in my family. Just pay me what we

agreed on and not one penny over the going rate for my expertise, thank you very much!"

"I didn't mean anything by that, Lana, I promise you. I was joking."

"I know that," Lana assured her. "You were just having fun, something that has been missing from my life for a while now. But I do still recognize it when I see it."

Lana wiped the tears from the corners of her eyes. She wasn't wasting any more tears on men like Gary Randall or Jeremy. "So, no apology needed."

Gia brightened. As she wrote the check, she said, "Have you ever thought of getting out of town for a while? Just for a change of scenery? I mean, why subject yourself to the likes of Gary Randall when you could be elsewhere?"

"Just stubborn, I guess," Lana told her as she accepted the check. "I haven't done anything wrong and I'm not going to let them chase me out of town."

Gia smiled at her. "I can understand that. I come from a lot of stubborn Greeks who never ever give up. But everybody needs a break sometime. Isn't there any place you go that instantly puts you in a peaceful state of mind?"

Home, was the first thought in Lana's head, the Outer Banks of North Carolina. She had grown up on the northernmost tip of Cape Hatteras Island where the people were tough and resilient like the land. Her dad used to say living in the Outer Banks was equivalent to going through the trials of Hercules. Hurricane season in the Outer Banks was oftentimes treacherous. The Atlantic Ocean was a cauldron and battered the area, wiped it clean and afforded Mother Nature another opportunity to start fresh. The storms were like life's tribulations, if you survived them you grew stronger.

"That would be the Outer Banks of North Carolina where I was born and raised," Lana told Gia.

"Then go home!" said Gia triumphantly.

"And look like a failure?" Lana said. "No, I'm not going home until I'm firmly back on my feet. That means not until my business is going well again. Or that bastard Jeremy gets caught and pays for what he did."

"Girlfriend, I think you have too much pride," Gia said frankly. "If I were in your situation, I'd be home in the bosom of my family getting as much support as I could. My family was poor but we loved each other! Is that it? You don't think your dad wants you there?"

Lana had to laugh. "Just the opposite," she told Gia. "If my dad had his way I would never have left Pea Island."

"Damn it!" Aaron Braithwaite spat out as he struggled to pull the kayak onto the beach. What had he been thinking taking Bowser fishing with him? He laughed at his ill-conceived decision. The two-year-old yellow Lab had gotten so excited when Aaron had landed a five-pound redfish that he tried to grab the fish in his jaws as Aaron pulled the hook out of the fish's mouth. Aaron had jerked around, trying to prevent the fish from winding up as dog food and had lost his balance. It was a good thing they weren't too far from shore that fine July morning. Man, dog and fish wound up in the ocean. Used to being dunked, Aaron had managed to get the kayak righted, and he and Bowser back on board. The fish unfortunately ended up back in its element, the sea.

"Next time, you stay home," he said to Bowser who looked up at him and wagged his tail. The dog whined plaintively as if he knew his master was berating him and he had something to say in his defense.

Aaron laughed. "So, you think I'm being unjust, do you? Well, you weren't the one who had to save both our asses."

Bowser whined again. He went up to Aaron and licked his hand.

"Okay, I know you're sorry," Aaron said. "And I admit I should have known a kayak was no place for a dog. Let's get home and get dry." The temperature was in the lower sixties and the wind was blowing pretty fiercely. Before long he would be chilled to the bone.

He began walking toward the three-story beach house only 150 feet away. The house had weathered many lashings from Outer Banks storms. Gray with white trim, it had multiple decks and, due to the big porthole-like windows, from a distance looked like a ship that had run aground.

Aaron smiled. When he was a fisherman he never would have been able to afford such a house. But now that he was a mystery writer, and a very successful one, he lived very well. Once again, every time he thought of how happy he was his mind took him to his daughter whose life, by contrast, was not a happy one.

The father in him wanted to demand that she come home. The realist knew that demanding anything of Lana, who was as stubborn as he was, was a sure way of getting her to dig her feet in and refuse to budge.

It was his fault. After his wife, Mariette, had died in an accident when Lana was eight he had raised her to be independent. Afraid that if he should die Lana would be left helpless, he stressed strength and determination within her. He taught her everything he knew about fishing and, a runner himself, he introduced her to the sport and was surprised when she took to it and ran circles around him.

Aside from fishing and running, Lana knew as much about the flora and fauna of Pea Island, parts of which were a nature reserve, as he did. If need be, she could live off the land for the rest of her life. Admittedly he had gone overboard with the survivalist agenda, but he was secure in the notion that his daughter could take care of herself in a pinch. This thing with Jeremy Corday, though, was not a physical challenge. It was something that ate away at her heart and soul. He feared more for her now than ever before in her thirty-two years.

"Mr. Braithwaite?"

Aaron had been so engrossed in his thoughts that he hadn't noticed the tall, broad-shouldered man standing at the foot of the house's front stairs.

He was wearing a dark suit, white shirt and tie. Aaron glanced down at his shoes, which were highly polished black wingtips. A government man, Aaron deduced. His mind first traveled to his taxes. Nah, he'd never cheated on his taxes. He didn't have a problem giving the government its fair share of his earnings.

The guy removed his shades and smiled at him. "You are Aaron Braithwaite, aren't you?"

Aaron chuckled. "Last time I checked, I was."

Bowser approached the stranger and growled softly. Not an aggressive show of dislike, but more of an inquisitive act. The guy held his hand out to Bowser who sniffed it and, deciding he was okay, licked it. The man gave him a fond ruffle of the fur on the top of his head for his efforts.

"Nice Lab," said the stranger.

"There's an old blues song that says 'Don't pat my dog and don't hug my woman,'" Aaron told the guy. "I don't have a woman around for you to get familiar with, so would you mind introducing yourself?"

"Oh, I'm sorry," said the man with an easy smile. "My name is Tennison Isles, and I'm with the FBI."

"FBI, IRS," mumbled Aaron. "Had to be one or the other."

"Excuse me?" Ten said, having not heard Aaron clearly.

"Nothing," said Aaron. "May I see some ID?"

Ten showed him his badge and picture ID.

After making a careful perusal of the items, Aaron met Ten's eyes. "What does the FBI want with me?"

"Hopefully, your cooperation," said Ten.

"Come on up," Aaron told him.

Fifteen minutes later, Aaron was in dry clothes, Bowser was fairly dry having been rubbed down with a warm towel and the two men were sitting across from each other in the spacious living room drinking strong coffee.

"I'm listening," Aaron said.

Ten told him what the Bureau wanted to do, with his help. Aaron listened intently. After he'd finished, Ten waited for Aaron's reaction to his proposal.

To his surprise Aaron said, "My doctor has been trying to get me to go into the hospital for a series of stress tests on my heart. Now is as good a time as any, I guess."

The next day, Lana received a phone call from Gladys Easterbrook, her father's closest neighbor. Gladys and Henry Easterbrook ran a bed-and-breakfast out of their huge beach house. "Aaron's in the hospital. It's his heart. That old reprobate told me not to call you, but I think a daughter has the right to know when her daddy's sick."

It had been a genius move on Aaron's part to have Gladys do the phoning. Everyone in Dare County knew Gladys had a talent for melodrama. She was the first person to start crying at every wedding and she hadn't missed a funeral, whether she knew the person or not, in the last thirty years. Just the sound of her angst-ridden Southern drawl got Lana moving in the direction of her hometown.

Gladys told her that her father was in the hospital in Kitty Hawk, the nearest hospital with full diagnostic services.

Lana had known Gladys Easterbrook nearly all her life and there was no reason to distrust her. However, she tried her father's cell phone anyway. There was no answer.

This heightened her fear and she immediately called the airport to book a flight home.

Chapter 3

Lana arrived at Norfolk International Airport at noon the following day. Once she departed the plane she looked everywhere for Gladys Easterbrook. She had tried to talk the older woman out of driving all the way to the airport when she could just rent a car and drive directly to the hospital. But Gladys had insisted.

"Mrs. Lana Braithwaite-Corday?" said a masculine voice behind her.

Lana spun around and peered up into the face of a gorgeous giant. He had burnt-caramel skin and eyes that were so dark brown they looked black. High cheekbones, a strong, masculine chin and a clean-shaven jaw added to his appeal. The neatly shorn hair on his well-shaped head was dark brown and its texture was wavy. She had this inane thought that when he was a boy, and his mother had let him grow it out, it must have fallen to his shoulders in thick spirals. He was wearing jeans, athletic shoes and a T-shirt with the University of Virginia emblem on the front. Her first thought after being confronted by all that hotness was, *Oh, God, not a reporter way down here!* True, he wasn't wearing a suit or shoving a microphone at her, but he was definitely TV-ready.

She brushed past him, clutching her shoulder bag and a small carry-on bag close to her side, as she headed for the exit. "Bug off. I've said all I'm going to say to the media."

"Your dad sent me to pick you up," the stranger called. "Miss Gladys's back is acting up today."

Lana stopped in her tracks and turned to regard him with a surprised expression on her face. She knew Miss Gladys often had back problems. "Who *are* you?" she asked tightly.

"Tennison West," Ten said, holding out a big hand for her to shake. "I'm a filmmaker working on a documentary about your father."

Lana briefly shook his hand, her eyes still locked with his as if she were trying to discern whether or not she could trust him by the intensity of her gaze.

"You got a driver's license?" she asked cautiously.

Ten showed her his driver's license which stated he was Tennison West and he lived in Washington, D.C. The bureau had established a whole new identity for him. They had even set up a website for him replete with samples of the past documentaries he'd produced.

They hadn't prepared him for Lana, though. Ten felt a bit vulnerable under her scrutiny. He had seen her only in photographs and in videos. He had read about her life in reports given to him by agents he'd assigned to observe her. To be this near, smelling her perfume, a light, enticing floral scent, was entirely different. He could feel the warmth emanating from her denim-clad body and it ignited his senses.

He attempted to turn them off, though. He was here only because he had a hunch that as soon as Lana arrived in the Outer Banks, she would be followed. The only way to find the person potentially trailing her was to be with her as much as possible. He had to be extremely observant, which meant he couldn't allow emotions to cloud his mind or judgment.

"That's odd," Lana commented as she handed him back his driver's license. "Dad didn't mention you the last time we talked. How long have you been working with him on this documentary?"

Ten smiled warmly. "Actually, he hasn't signed on the dotted line yet. I went to see your father, explained what I wanted to do, he then passed out and I took him directly to the emergency room."

Lana stared up at him, startled. "We're wasting time. There's still a two-hour drive to Kitty Hawk!"

She sprinted from the terminal with Ten close behind, shouting, "He told me to tell you not to worry. Wait, don't you have any luggage?"

Lana didn't slow down in her headlong rush. "No, no luggage. I was in a hurry. Where's your car?" She didn't have time to explain to this stranger that she had a closet full of clothes in her old bedroom at her dad's house. It saved her from having to pack for her frequent trips home.

Ten got in front, and then reached back for her hand. "If you'll allow me?"

They jogged hand in hand to the black SUV that was waiting in visitor parking. Ten helped her inside, then went around to the driver's side and got in.

He turned to her as he started the engine. "There's no need to panic. I overheard the doctor telling him he has a little arrhythmia. Nothing he can't live with for a very long time."

That was news to Lana. Her father didn't have any health problems that she knew of. He was sixty-two and he still ran practically every day. He'd never smoked and he drank in moderation. The only vice he had was too much shellfish, which could be high in cholesterol. The man loved shrimp and lobster; he could devour steamed soft-shell crabs by the bucketful.

As he drove out of the parking lot, Ten noticed a short dark-skinned man with thick dreadlocks surreptitiously snap a photo of them with his cell phone. He smiled with satisfaction. Earlier, while he was waiting for Lana to arrive, he had seen the same man rubber-necking when the passengers from Lana's flight were disembarking. The guy had obviously been waiting for someone and, when his gaze had fallen on Lana, he'd taken a couple of photos of her. Ten had then im-mediately taken photos of *him*.

"Did you see that?" Lana asked.

"See what?" Ten casually said.

"That guy just took our picture. Why would he do that?" The picture-snapper was dressed shabbily in dirty jeans, stained white athletic shoes and a faded long-sleeved shirt. Not the basic attire of a reporter. And Lana didn't believe she was gossip-worthy enough for grungy paparazzi to have any interest in her. Be-sides, wouldn't they use professional-quality cameras instead of a cell-phone camera?

"Have you ever seen him before?" Ten wanted to know. He watched as the guy got into a late-model Toyota Corolla. He made a mental note of the car's tag number.

"No," Lana responded tiredly.

"Are you a celebrity or something?" she asked, looking sideways at him.

Ten laughed. "In no way, shape or form," he said. "I work behind the camera. Are you?"

Lana gave him a suspicious look. If he'd done his homework on her father before approaching him about doing a documentary on him, wouldn't he have found out that Aaron Braithwaite's only child was married to one of the most notorious frauds of the century? Or maybe she was giving Jeremy too much credit. Yes, he was public enemy number one in San Francisco but how many people had ever heard of him on a global scale?

"I would have to say no to that," she said dryly.

"Maybe he just likes taking photos of beautiful women," Ten said, smiling at her.

Lana laughed. "Now you're being ridiculous."

"Beautiful and modest, too," Ten said admiringly.

"Just keep your eyes on the road, buster," Lana jokingly told him. But his compliment had relaxed her and made her laugh. God knew she could use a good laugh.

"Yes, ma'am," said Ten good-naturedly, focusing on his driving.

The traffic from the airport was congested but once they got on the interstate, driving was a cinch. They made small talk all the way to Kitty Hawk, North Carolina, where Aaron had been admitted into the hospital.

"Nice little town," Ten said. "There's no traffic to speak of."

"Your first time here?" asked Lana, peering at him with a small smile on her lips.

"Your dad and I have had many conversations over the phone but this is my first visit to the Outer Banks," Ten told her.

"Oh, then I should at least give you a little background on Kitty Hawk," Lana offered pleasantly. "The town's best known for being the site of the Wright brothers' test ground for their first controlled airplane flights. Although that was misinformation because the actual site's about four miles from Kitty Hawk in sand dunes the locals refer to as Kill Devil Hills. Kitty Hawk today is a pleasant town with a population of about 3300 residents. It gets its fair share of visitors, though, especially in the warmer months. The beaches here are very pristine."

"You could probably say that about all of the beaches in the Outer Banks," Ten ventured. "This area looks like it's washed clean by Mother Nature on a regular basis."

Lana laughed softly. "That's a nice way to put it. A lot of people out here have very strong feelings about keeping the Outer Banks as close to the way nature made it as possible. So when developers start making noise about building huge resorts to attract more tourists, and so forth, you can bet you're going to get some opposition. Then, too, nature has a way of keeping the Outer Banks pure. We build roads, nature floods them. We build bridges and the ocean erodes them. Sometimes it can be a hard life, but like Dad says, you've got to be tough to be an Outer Banker."

Ten noted the fond tone in her voice. How her smile never wavered as she talked of her beloved home. If she loved it so much, what had kept her away for so long?

Why had it taken scheming from the FBI and her father to get her back here?

"Your father said you live in San Francisco," he said, instead of asking her what he really wanted to ask her.

"Yeah, my hus… I mean, I've lived there for about a decade now." She suddenly focused on something outside of the window.

They rode in silence. Ten let the husband comment slip. It wasn't his place to pry any further into her private life than he had to in order to get the job done. He felt acutely sympathetic toward her. Now that he'd met her, he believed more than ever that she had not been privy to Jeremy Corday's illegal business dealings.

Once they were in the city of Kitty Hawk, the trip through town and out to North Croatan Highway where Albemarle Health's Regional Medical Center was located took only fifteen minutes. Ten pulled up to the entrance.

"Go on in," he said. "I'll find a parking space and meet you inside."

She looked at him with those beautiful brown eyes and he fairly melted. "Thank you, Mr. West, but if you have someplace else to be I can get home from here."

"On the contrary, Mrs. Corday," he told her calmly, "it would be my pleasure to wait and drive you home. I promised your father I'd look after you and I always keep my promises."

Lana didn't know what to say to that. A helpful man who always kept his promises?

She didn't have time to argue the point with him. Her father needed her.

"Okay then," she relented with a smile. She got out, closed the door and hurried inside. Ten watched her for a moment as she gracefully walked toward the steel-framed glass wall that encased the automatic doors. His heart was still thudding from the impact of her smile.

He blew air between full lips as he drove away to locate a parking spot. "Lord, this is not going to be an easy assignment."

"Keep running," Dr. Sanjay Khan said to Aaron, his lilting voice kind. "Just don't overdo it. At your age a couple of miles a day is enough. I'm not even going to prescribe any medication because your arrhythmia doesn't call for it. I do want you on the aspirin regimen and you need to watch your cholesterol more closely."

Aaron, lying in bed, one arm behind his head as he sat propped up on pillows, laughed softly. "Doc, you're not going to take my butter away, are you? What am I going to dip my lobster in?"

Dr. Khan laughed, too. "Butter and lobster, no wonder your cholesterol's high. I want you on olive oil and good omega-3 seafood like salmon."

"I hate the taste of both," Aaron complained.

"You'll just have to get used to them," Lana spoke up as she entered the room.

She walked straight over to her father, and kissed

him on the cheek, then greeted Dr. Khan with a warm smile and a hearty hello.

Dr. Khan, in his late forties, was about her height and looked fit in his white physician's coat with a white shirt and black tie underneath, black slacks and sturdy black oxfords. His dark liquid eyes lit up at her hello. "You must be Lana," he said. "Your father has been expecting you."

"Yes," said Lana, smiling warmly. She lovingly gazed at Aaron. "How is he, Doctor?"

Aaron started to say something, and Lana shushed him. He fell quiet, his face a mass of grins. He was so delighted to have her home, he didn't care that she was being bossy, as usual.

Dr. Khan patiently went over Aaron's condition with Lana. She asked questions and he answered them to her satisfaction. When she felt there was no more to learn on the subject, she thanked Dr. Khan who told them he had to go but he would be back in the morning at which time he would let Aaron know if he could go home. The doctor advised that there were still test results that hadn't come in yet.

Alone with her father, Lana fell on him and hugged him tightly. Then she rose and peered into his beloved face, a face that was a pleasant reminder of their shared genetics. He also had a dash of freckles across the bridge of his nose. And if not for his sixty-two years his hair would have been the same red-brown. Today, it was pure white. His skin was a deep golden-brown due to the sun, wind and salt air that he lived in every day. She loved the crinkles around his brown eyes and the bushy white eyebrows above them.

"I've missed you," she said. Tears came to her eyes in spite of her attempt to keep them at bay.

Aaron squeezed her hand. "I'm fine, sweetheart. You know nothing gets me down for long."

"I do," she said, trying to sound upbeat. "But the older I get the more I realize that you're not getting any younger, either. That's a scary thought. What would I do if anything ever happened to you? It's not like I have a huge family to fall back on."

Her mother, Mariette, had a sister, Dorothy—Aunt Dottie to Lana—who lived in Florida. However her father was the last of the Braithwaites in North Carolina. There were some distant cousins in Massachusetts whom he never heard from. He and Mariette had wanted to have more children but they'd only been blessed with Lana.

Lana wanted to have children with Jeremy but he had convinced her to wait a few more years. He said he wanted to enjoy their time as a couple for the first five years of their marriage. Then he said they could have a child or two. If given the choice of having Jeremy's child with her now or him, Lana would have chosen the child. Just because Jeremy had proven unreliable and less than honest didn't mean his child would have been tainted. The child would have been loved by her beyond measure.

"You're only thirty-two. There's still time to have children and make me a granddaddy," Aaron reminded her, his eyes twinkling with merriment.

Lana laughed. "In case you haven't heard, my husband's a fugitive and I'm in the process of divorcing him."

"A wise decision, as I told you over the phone," her father said. He patted the side of the bed and Lana sat down. He hugged her close. "Lana, there's only one way to get on with your life when something as devastating as what happened to you occurs. You have to keep moving forward. You had plans before you met Jeremy. Some of them you put on hold for him. Becoming a mother was one of them. Jeremy's not in the picture anymore. You have the reins. Don't allow his behavior to define the rest of your life. We can't control other people's behavior. All we can do is control how we react to it."

"And even that's hard to do," Lana said.

"Have you ever noticed how the important things in life are always difficult to accomplish? That's because God wants you to recognize the blessings in life when you're presented with them, and appreciate them."

Lana looked at her father with a deadpan expression. "Are you saying my experience has been a blessing?"

"Now you know what kind of man you married. It would have been worse if you had been with him twenty years instead of five and all of this happened," Aaron said reasonably.

"It stings pretty badly right now," Lana asserted.

"Of course it does, but eventually they will find him, and you'll be able to face him and tell him to go to hell and you'll live through it. You're tougher than you think."

Lana knew her father was right. After she had admitted to herself that Jeremy had faked his death and run away, she had spent weeks beating up on herself for being so gullible and allowing herself to love a man like him. Now, if she ever saw him again she believed she would stomp on him. She was that angry with him.

She smiled at her dad. "What about your health and you being in the hospital for the first time in your life. Is that a blessing?"

Aaron's smile grew wider. "It got you home, didn't it?"

Lana rolled her eyes. "You never quit."

"Never, baby girl."

Lana stood up. She looked around the room. Flowers were on every available surface. "Your women?" she joked, referring to the number of bouquets.

"Well, you know…" he said with no modesty whatsoever. "What can I say? There are more women than men in our age group. Somebody has to take up the slack."

Lana went to read a few of the cards attached to the bouquets. Sure enough, they were from females.

Some names she recognized, some she didn't. One in particular was of interest to her. It was her high school English teacher, Miss Ellen Newman.

"Miss Newman, Daddy? You're seeing Miss Newman?" She couldn't keep the surprise out of her voice.

"She's an attractive woman," Aaron said. "And we share certain interests." He raised his eyebrows in a lascivious manner, which made Lana guffaw.

"I don't want to hear anything about Miss Newman's certain interests," Lana hurriedly told him.

"I was just going to say she likes going fishing, too," Aaron said innocently.

"I'll bet," Lana said dryly. She turned to face him again after reading the message on another card: *Get well soon, Tiger!* It had been signed by another female admirer whose name she didn't recognize.

"Maybe giving up butter and lobster aren't the only things you should think about letting go," she said with a laugh.

"I'd give up the shellfish before I gave up the ladies," vowed Aaron through a smile.

Chapter 4

Ten was waiting when Lana exited her father's hospital room. She looked up, and he was there as if out of nowhere. She smiled at him, and was reminded of the fact that she hadn't gotten the chance to question her father about this good-looking man. She'd wanted to know his opinion of him.

"Oh, Mr. West," she said, "there you are. Look, really, I can get home from here. Don't trouble yourself any longer."

"Are we going to go over that again?" Ten asked with a smile that brought out the dimples in both cheeks. Lana's heart did a little flip-flop. *Oh, calm down,* she told the out-of-control muscle. But then, it wasn't as if it'd gotten much exercise lately. Not since she'd relegated the male species to a genus lower than an earthworm.

It was unkind to be rude, though, so she tolerated his enthusiasm.

She began walking toward the bank of elevators here on the fourth floor. Ten fell into step beside her. "How's your dad?"

"Cracking jokes with the best of them," she said. "If I didn't know better I'd think this is some ruse just to get me home. I wouldn't put it past him."

Ten squirmed a little when she said that. Guilt wasn't an emotion that he had time for though. Lana's presence could very well flush out that rat Jeremy Corday.

He grimaced. Okay, where had the name-calling come from? Formerly, he had thought of Jeremy Corday only as the subject of an FBI dragnet. No personal feelings had entered into it. Now all of a sudden he was attaching derogatory labels to him? Maybe it was because he had not before been so close to someone Corday had damaged with his underhanded behavior. His sympathy for Lana was growing by leaps and bounds.

He regarded Lana with a quizzical look in his eyes. "You're joking, right? Would it take something as elaborate as that to get you to come home?"

For a moment he thought he'd overstepped his bounds because Lana simply stared up at him without saying a word for quite some time, even though it was probably only a few seconds. Then she sighed and said, "I don't know you. You're doing a story on my dad and I don't want to say anything that might end up in that story. I'm sure you understand."

The elevator doors opened and he and Lana watched as several people got off the conveyance. He was now alone with her and he pressed the call button for the lobby. "I'm off the clock," he said. "I promise you as a journalist and, better yet, as an honorable human being, that anything you say will go no further than right here, right now."

Lana laughed quietly. "Now see, here we are with the same conundrum. I don't know you well enough to trust that I can take you at your word." She'd had her fill of charming men. Not to mention, Jeremy, who had a way of making you divulge everything about yourself until you were laid bare.

Her eyes narrowed. "Why don't you spill your guts to me?" she challenged.

Ten shrugged as if that was no tall order. "What do you want to know?"

"Just the basics," she said, eyes raking over his face.

"Okay. I'm thirty-five, single, I live in D.C. but I was born in Virginia," he placed his hand on his chest. "I attended the University of Virginia where I earned a master's degree in literature."

"Literature?" asked Lana skeptically. "What can you do with a master's in literature?"

"Exactly," said Ten, grinning. "So I parlayed my

interest in filmmaking into a career. I love books and writers. I focus on literary themes."

"Do your parents also love books and writers?"

"Not particularly. Why?" he asked out of curiosity.

"They named you Tennison after Tennyson, the poet, right?"

Ten laughed. "That's a funny story. Let me preface this by saying my parents really love kids."

Lana burst out laughing. A ridiculous reason had come to her of why he'd been named Tennison, but she had a hard time believing it. "No," she interrupted him, "Don't tell me you're the tenth son: Ten is son… Tennison?"

"Not the tenth son, but I am the tenth child, and the last. Thank God. My parents have six sons and four daughters. I'm the baby of the family."

Lana was laughing so hard tears were rolling down her cheeks. "I'm sorry if I'm being insensitive. Just the notion that your parents named you Tennison because you were their tenth child is so…sweet."

"Nice save," Ten said, laughing along with her. "But you're being too kind. It's my guess that by the tenth child, with two sets of twins among them, they were running out of names and brain cells. Naming me Tennison is an easy way to remember I'm number ten."

Lana wiped her tears away. "Do you still have all your brothers and sisters?"

"Yeah," said Ten. "And my parents. Believe me,

when we get together for family reunions it's quite a production."

"How many nieces and nephews do you have?" Lana asked.

"Last count, twenty-seven," Ten said without hesitation. "I'm the only one of my nine brothers and sisters who hasn't had any children."

"You're a lucky man to have such a big family," Lana said, smiling up at him.

They arrived in the lobby. Stepping out of the elevator, Ten glimpsed the same man they'd seen at the airport. He was sitting in the lounge area pretending to be engrossed in a magazine.

Ten didn't allow his gaze to linger in case Lana, who had recently proven very perceptive, caught him observing the stranger. Then, he would have to explain himself.

"Now, will you let me drive you home?" he asked Lana.

Before Lana could reply, a shrill female scream erupted from the throat of a petite African-American woman bearing down on them. "Lana!"

Ten couldn't believe his ears when Lana let go with a piercing scream of her own. "Bobbi Lee!"

The two women hugged there in the middle of the huge lobby, their exclamations echoing loudly off the high ceiling and marble floor.

"I heard you were in town," Bobbi Lee said, her pretty face shining with affection.

She was five-five to Lana's five-nine and she had a pleasantly plump figure. Her long black hair was pulled back in a ponytail and she was wearing green scrubs and white athletic shoes.

After she'd let go of Bobbi Lee, Lana took a good look at her. "What is this, a new career?" The last time she'd seen her old high school friend and fellow cheerleader, she was working as a receptionist at a dentist's office.

"I'm a registered nurse now," Bobbi Lee told her proudly, "as of the first of the year!"

"Congratulations," Lana said with warmth. "How do you like it?"

"I love it," said Bobbi Lee. Then she looked up at Ten. "Oh, I'm sorry if I interrupted something."

"Bobbi Lee Erskine, this is Tennison West."

Bobbi Lee and Ten exchanged hellos after which Bobbi Lee said, "Yes, I heard you were making a movie about Mr. Aaron."

Small towns, Ten thought. *I'm here for three days and I'm already the subject of gossip.*

"Actually, it's a documentary," Lana provided.

"Well, you know Miss Gladys can't get her details right to save her life," Bobbi Lee said with a laugh. "Momma still works for her and Momma gets the gossip from her and by the time she passes it on to me the facts are a bit screwy."

"How *is* Miss Louise?" asked Lana.

"Past the age of retirement and with no plans to retire," Bobbi Lee quipped. Her facial expression turned sober. "I know Mr. Aaron's here having tests done on his heart. I'm not keeping you from him, am I?"

"No, we were just leaving after visiting him. He's going to be just fine."

"I'm glad to hear it," Bobbi Lee said enthusiastically. "I was heading home myself. Can I give you a lift? It'd give us a chance to catch up."

"Oh, thanks, Bobbi Lee, but I've already got a ride home," Lana said regrettably.

Ten who had been watching the man who had been watching Lana out of the corner of his eye saw his opportunity to tail him. "Don't give it a second thought. Go with Bobbi Lee. I'll call you later to see if you need anything. I'm staying at Miss Gladys's place, so I won't be far away."

"Okay," Lana reluctantly said. She still wasn't a hundred percent trusting of Ten quite yet but he seemed nice enough. "Thanks for your help today."

Ten murmured, "My pleasure," as Lana and Bobbi Lee walked toward the exit. He then took out his cell phone and pretended to check his messages.

"I'm so glad you're home, we're celebrating our anniversary this Saturday and you're invited," he faintly heard Bobbi Lee tell Lana.

But as soon as Lana and Bobbi Lee walked through the automatic doors the guy in the lobby put down his magazine, got up and followed. Ten consequently followed the guy.

* * *

To Ten's surprise the man didn't follow Bobbi Lee's sporty SUV. Instead the man's Corolla headed back in the direction of downtown Kitty Hawk. Less than fifteen minutes later he parked in front of an old building that must have been part of Kitty Hawk's original downtown. It housed three separate businesses as far as Ten could see, a beauty salon; a barbershop; and a detective agency. He watched as the man got out of his car and used a key to enter the detective agency. *Must be a one-man operation,* Ten thought.

Ten didn't stop. He drove straight to Hatteras Island where the rest of his team were staying in a hotel only a few miles from the Braithwaite house. Ten was staying at Gladys Easterbrook's bed-and-breakfast so that if he were needed he would be within walking distance of the Braithwaites' house. While his team kept the newfound private detective under surveillance, he would keep an eye on Lana.

Each night before bed Lana removed her locket necklace and opened it. Inside were photos of her parents. Her mother on the right side, her father on the left. When Jeremy had given her the heavy, expensive piece of gold jewelry as a fifth-anniversary gift, he had put a photo of himself on one side and a photo of them on their wedding day on the other. But since his disappearance she had removed their photos. She was rarely without the locket. Only when she show-

ered, worked out or slept did she remove it. She smiled
as she looked at her mother's face. Like her, Mariette
had not been what some people described as beautiful. However, she'd had the most expressive brown
eyes and her smile came directly from the heart. Lana
had her smile.

She placed the locket on the nightstand and settled
down in bed. Bowser, who wasn't allowed on the furniture, somehow wangled a spot across the foot of the
bed. She yawned and turned out the light. "G'night,
boy," she murmured. Bowser whined softly in response.

It didn't bother her being alone in such a big house.
Bowser was there, and her father also had a good security system, which she'd engaged before going upstairs to bed.

A couple of minutes after her head hit the pillow,
she was fast asleep.

A little after three in the morning she was awakened by low but menacing growling from Bowser. Her
eyes sprang open to the pitch-black of the bedroom.
She reached over to turn on the lamp atop the nightstand, and instead her hand touched the arm of someone. She screamed, and leaped for the other side of the
bed, scrambling to her feet. Bowser was already on the
floor, chasing whomever she had touched in the dark.
She heard heavy steps bounding down the stairs. She
switched on the light, her eyes adjusting and quickly
scanning the room. The top drawer of the bureau where

she kept her jewelry when she stayed here was hanging open but nothing else looked out of place.

She could hear Bowser barking downstairs. Common sense told her she should not chase after a burglar. Nowadays criminals were getting bolder and sometimes kicking in the front door of homes, and brutally attacking the families.

She picked up the receiver of the phone on the nightstand. There was a dial tone, so fortunately whoever had broken in hadn't tried to sabotage the phone line. She dialed 911 and reported a break-in while simultaneously trying to listen to what was going on downstairs. Then it dawned on her: she hadn't heard a thing during the assault on the house. If not for Bowser's growling she would have probably slept through it all. That meant the burglar knew the security code to her father's house. How had he gotten access to that code?

The 911 operator, a woman with a thick Southern accent, advised her that the police would be at her address in less than five minutes and to lock her bedroom door. Lana didn't know why it hadn't occurred to her to lock the door, but she walked over, and followed the woman's instructions.

She stayed on the phone with the operator until she heard sirens outside. "They're here," she said to the operator.

"Good," replied the operator. "Stay put. More than likely your door was left open when the perpetrator ran away."

She was right. About thirty seconds later a police-man was at Lana's bedroom door.

"Miss Corday, my name is Officer Edwards. I'm with the Hatteras Island Police Department. We have a report of a break-in at this residence. Are you all right?"

Meanwhile about a quarter of a mile down the beach, Gladys had gotten up to get a glass of water from downstairs. When she happened to glance out her kitchen window, she saw the police cruisers' lights flashing in the direction of the Braithwaite house. The lights were so brilliant that she didn't even need the assistance of her trusty telescope. She didn't want to wake Henry, who had insomnia and needed every bit of sleep he could get, so she went and knocked on Ten's door.

A groggy Ten staggered to the door and opened it wearing only boxers. Gladys was clearly startled by his near-nakedness for a moment but quickly regained her composure. He'd bet she hadn't seen a male body like his up close in a month of Sundays! "There's somethin' goin' on at Aaron's place," she blurted. "Police or am-bulances, I can't tell which, are down there!"

That's all Ten needed to hear. "I'll check it out," he told her and firmly closed the door to hurriedly get dressed. Two minutes later he was sprinting down the beach.

Gladys went onto the deck to watch him run. "Be

still my heart! That's one fine specimen of manhood."
She laughed out loud. "On second thought, *don't* be
still, my heart. At my age one mustn't tempt fate…"
Her voice trailed off.

Ten ran straight into the Braithwaite house. There
were two patrol cars parked out front. Four officers
in total were there. Two outside on the porch, looking around as if they were trying to ascertain how the
perpetrator had entered the house, and the other two
were inside talking to Lana.

When Lana looked up and saw Ten, he could see
the relief on her face from recognizing someone she
knew. "Tennison," she breathed. "I forgot you were
staying at Miss Gladys's."

He was surprised when she approached him for
comfort and was even more surprised by how natural
it felt to wrap his arms around her.

The policemen, however, were giving him suspicious looks.

"It's okay, he's staying with my neighbor down the
beach," Lana told them. "She runs a bed-and-breakfast.
I know him."

"What happened?" Ten asked.

The lead officer, Officer Edwards, then gave an account of Lana's statement, after which he wanted to
know if Ten had encountered anyone on his run over
here to see what the commotion was about.

"No," Ten said regrettably, "there was no one on
the beach."

"Did you hear any car doors slamming or an engine starting after the perpetrator fled?" Officer Edwards asked Lana.

She shook her head.

"He must have left his vehicle several blocks away," Ten suggested. "If Lana didn't hear anything until he was already in her bedroom, stealth was his objective." He looked around. "And from the lack of physical evidence of a break-in, he must have known how to get around the security system, like Lana said."

Officer Edwards twisted the end of his bushy black moustache. "Can you tell me of anyone besides your father and yourself who would know the code?"

Lana couldn't think of anyone. Surely her father hadn't given it to any of his lady friends. That was just asking for trouble, the fatal attraction kind. "Only the people who work for the security firm," she said. "But you should talk to my father, Officer. I don't live here. I'm just visiting."

Officer Edwards sighed with resignation. It was apparent to Lana that he was hoping for more of a lead to go on. "Excuse me a moment," he said, and walked outside to confer with his partners in uniform, beckoning to the other officer in the room as he went past him.

In their absence, Ten asked, "Are you sure nothing's missing?"

Lana's hand automatically went to her throat since she was so used to the locket being around her neck.

She immediately felt its absence. "My locket!" she cried, and took off running for the stairs. Ten followed.

She breathed a sigh of relief when she saw the locket, safe on the nightstand where she'd left it that night. "Thank God he didn't get this," she said as she slipped it into the pocket of her bathrobe.

They then headed back downstairs where Officer Edwards was waiting to speak with Lana. "Miss Corday," he said gravely, "we could find no means by which the perpetrator entered your house, therefore we will have to conclude, at least for the time being, that he had a key and knew your security codes. You're positive you engaged the system before going to bed?"

"I'm sure," Lana told him.

"I hear your father is a successful author. This guy could be a deranged fan or something. He is definitely not your run-of-the-mill break-and-enter kind of criminal. This took some finesse. But we'll find him. Until we do, we'll patrol the area. I would suggest, however, that you not stay here tonight. Do you have somewhere you could go?"

"Officer," Ten spoke up. "Mrs. Corday won't be alone. I'll stay with her."

Officer Edwards looked to Lana for her approval or disapproval of the suggestion. She nodded. "Thank you, Officer. Between Mr. West and Bowser I should be safe."

Bowser stood by her side, wagging his tail. She rubbed his head.

Officer Edwards smiled down at Bowser. "That's a good dog you've got there." Earlier Lana had told him how Bowser had chased the burglar out of the house.

Lana escorted Officer Edwards to the door, and called her thanks to the other officers.

She closed and locked the door, then set the alarm once again.

Turning to Ten, she said, "I know I'm not going to get back to sleep now. Want to watch one of Dad's old movies?"

They settled on the couch in the living room and watched—in Lana's case, cried over—the 1934 version of *Imitation of Life* starring Louise Beavers and Claudette Colbert.

Lana made popcorn and raided her dad's stock of Coronas, his favorite beer. She rarely drank and was hoping the alcohol would put her to sleep. But Ten's company was so stimulating she didn't feel sleepy at all after downing a brew.

She burped daintily behind her hand after swallowing the last of the Corona. "Excuse me," she said.

"Please, Lana, I barely heard a sound," Ten joked. "Are all you Southern belles so genteel?"

"Southern belle?" asked Lana. "My daddy didn't raise no Southern belle!"

Ten grinned, getting into their give-and-take. They were both stretched out on the large eight-foot couch, their feet touching. Ten had on socks, Lana didn't. She still had on her bathrobe, under which was a rather skimpy nightgown. The thick cotton robe whose hem fell a couple inches past her knees covered it appropriately. Ten was enjoying the view of her shapely legs, though. Up until now he'd seen her only in jeans.

"What *did y*our daddy raise?" he asked, brows arched questioningly.

"I think he wanted a boy," Lana told him. "He taught me how to use a gun, to hunt, fish and swim. He even taught me how to be tough even when I really wanted to cry like a baby."

"You sound like Tucker Brady," Ten said.

Lana sat up straighter and regarded him with a new perspective. Tucker Brady was her father's most beloved character. Tucker was born and bred in the Outer Banks. His father had taught him to live off the land and to be resilient when faced with any obstacles. He was a detective in New York City but he used wiles he'd learned in the Outer Banks to catch criminals in an urban setting.

"You've read the Tucker Brady books?" she asked softly.

Ten laughed. "Of course I've read them. Would I have asked your dad if I could make a documentary about his life if I weren't a real fan?"

"I suppose not," Lana admitted. "It's just that it's so seldom I meet a man who reads."

"Is that a turn-on?" Ten asked playfully.

"It would be if I weren't a married woman," Lana

said, effectively pouring ice water on any thoughts of ardor on his part.

"I see," said Ten. His gaze rested on her ring finger. "From the moment I met you I couldn't help noticing you don't wear a wedding ring. I only referred to you as Mrs. Corday because your father *told* me you were married."

Lana slumped back on the couch. "That's a long story. The kind that would put a damper on what has, besides the obvious exception of a burglary, been a pretty pleasant night."

Ten smiled at that. He was glad she was loosening up and beginning to regard him as a friend. "I don't mean to pry, so if you don't want to tell me why you're not wearing your rings, it's okay."

Lana met his gaze. "I'm not wearing them because I don't even know where my husband is. To get the full story, all you have to do is put the name Jeremy Corday into any search engine."

Ten wasn't about to pretend he didn't know who Jeremy Corday was. He would be a pretty poor journalist if he hadn't thoroughly researched his subject, Aaron Braithwaite, before coming to the Outer Banks to interview him. That meant looking into his immediate family as well.

"You can relax," he said softly. "I know who Jeremy Corday is and I don't believe the hype the media has been spreading about you."

Lana didn't look surprised by his admission. Her

eyes never left his face. "I had a feeling you knew all along," she told him.

"How could you have guessed?" he asked cautiously.

"It was the way you looked at me...sympathetic, bordering on pity."

Ten was shocked. If that were the case, he was more competent in his undercover role than in his role as an agent. He wasn't supposed to allow his emotions to come to the forefront when dealing with subjects of an investigation.

"I'm sorry if you thought I pitied you," he said. "I don't. I do sympathize, though. I believed you when I'd heard you knew nothing about his criminal activities. The first rule of any con artist is to keep his moves close to his chest. It wouldn't make sense for him to tell you anything."

"Not only did he keep his business a secret from me," Lana said, "in essence, he kept himself a secret from me. Most of the details he told me about himself turned out to be untrue."

Lana told Ten about the time FBI agents had come to the house following the explosion on the yacht. He saw the scene unfold in his mind as she spoke.

Still an emotional wreck the following day, she had been crying when two agents arrived and asked if they could speak with her about Jeremy Corday. As they had sat on her designer sofa in her million-dollar home, overlooking San Francisco Bay, they told her of the various aliases Jeremy had used over the years. His real name was Jeremy, yes, but his real last name was Davis. Jeremy Davis had been born in Los Angeles, and he still had family there, a mother, a father and several brothers and sisters. Another lie, since he'd told her he had been an orphan and literally shuffled from one temporary home to another. Oh, and he had failed to mention that he had been married twice before. Apparently, he also had four children. No wonder he hadn't wanted more with her.

Lana released a weary sigh. She somehow felt better after letting all of that out. She smiled at Ten. "Just call me the bag lady, because, boy do I have plenty of baggage."

Seeing the sheer misery in her eyes caused Ten to truly hate Jeremy Corday in that moment.

This had now become personal to him. He moved closer and pulled her into his embrace.

She curled up to him, and relaxed in his arms, laying her head on his shoulder and closing her eyes. "I'm so tired."

"Then go to sleep," he said softly.

So she did.

Chapter 5

Lana was dreaming she was floating in the ocean looking up at a pale blue, cloudless sky. The water was warm and she could hear it lapping at her ears as she lay on the surface. Suddenly, a dolphin swam up to her and nudged her in the side with its nose. She didn't panic. It was as if the dolphin was an old friend and had simply come to play. She flipped over onto her stomach and reached for the dolphin, which nuzzled her face. But instead, she awoke to Bowser licking her face.

"I love you, but you could use a breath mint," she cried.

She was still on the couch where she'd fallen asleep in Ten's arms before dawn this morning. A throw had been placed over her. She sat up, and stretched. Bowser sat down on the floor beside her and patiently waited for her to acknowledge him. She knew it was time for his morning meal but he rarely rushed her. She wondered if he was this patient with her father when it came to mealtime.

She smelled coffee. Then she heard someone moving around in the kitchen, someone who was obviously looking for a frying pan or other cookware from the sound of it.

She got up and trudged into the kitchen where she saw Ten bent over, rummaging in the lower cabinets where her father kept his pots and pans.

"Good morning," she said as she walked into the kitchen. The clock on the wall above the sink read 8:13.

Ten looked as good this morning as he had last night. His dark-chocolate eyes lit up when he saw her. The stubble on his face just made him better-looking. No matter in the corners of his eyes, or dry-looking lips. She had hastily cleaned the corners of her eyes before strolling in, but she was sure her hair was sticking up on her head and that her lips were dry. A surreptitious intake of breath also revealed she had morning breath. *Just great,* she thought.

"Hey," he said with a smile. "I was going to cook breakfast for you but I couldn't find a frying pan."

She walked over and pulled open the drawer next to the gas cooktop. "Voila!" Her dad didn't store his frying pans below, he kept them in a drawer next to the stove for easy access, since he used them more often than the other pots and pans.

"Smart," Ten said with approval. He selected a medium-size skillet and put it atop a burner. "How do you like your eggs?"

"Any way you cook them," Lana said. "I'm not picky. Just don't put any salt on them. I think salt and sugar poison the system and should be avoided as much as possible. We already get enough of both in our food without adding more. Besides, I like the natural taste of food."

"Duly noted," Ten said as he spooned some butter into the skillet. "I see your dad uses real butter, not that imitation stuff."

"He's going on olive oil when he gets home from the hospital," Lana said.

"Kicking and screaming," Ten predicted.

"You can bet on that." Lana laughed. She then went to the pantry and grabbed a big bag of dry dog food and poured some into Bowser's bowl after which she mixed it with a can of organic dog food that looked like chunks of beef in gravy.

Bowser who was close by tore into the bowl as if he were starving. "Slow down," she chided with a laugh.

"So that's what he was trying to tell me," Ten said as he gently flipped fried eggs in the skillet. "He came up to me, and just sat down. After I ignored him he must have gone looking for you."

"Woke me up out of a great dream," Lana said with a mischievous smile.

"Oh, yeah?" said Ten. "Were you alone in it?"

"No, there was someone else there," she said.

"How were you dressed?"

"I was practically naked," Lana answered nonchalantly. She was putting fresh water into a bowl for Bowser as Ten slid the cooked eggs onto two plates.

"Were the both of you practically naked?"

"Dolphins don't wear clothes, so I guess he was *completely* naked," she said as she turned to look him in the eyes. "Gotcha!"

Ten laughed. "You're a tease."

"Just practicing my skills for the day when I start trusting the male sex again. That is, if that day ever comes," she said with an awkward grin. "Come on, let's eat, then I need to phone the hospital and see what time they're going to let Dad come home today."

They ate fried eggs, toast with strawberry jam and drank glasses of orange juice and cups of Jamaican coffee. They talked easily throughout the meal. Ten even told her past stories of his love life.

Lana assumed the role of advisor since she said she was an "unbiased onlooker with experience under her belt," which meant she'd been bruised and battered in the relationship game and was qualified to warn him of the pitfalls.

"You say the last woman you dated cheated on you

because of your need to travel for your job?" she asked, looking at him over the rim of her coffee mug.

"Yeah," Ten said, his gaze on her mouth. He was trying his best to stay aloof and unaffected by her magnetism but so far it had been a losing proposition. She exuded sexuality even in that bulky bathrobe, which hid every curve of her body.

It was in the way she pouted unconsciously, her mouth looking so enticing he could almost taste her lips. It was also in the curve of her neck, so graceful, and the symmetry of her clavicle, so damned sexy. Women didn't know how drawn a man could be to parts of their bodies they never gave a single thought to. A man craved more than breasts, legs and butts. A woman's back for example could be an invitation to sex for a man.

Ten had to stop himself. Lana had said something, but he'd missed it because he'd been so preoccupied wondering what was underneath her robe.

"I'm sorry?" he coaxed.

"I said your job isn't the reason she cheated on you. If I really like a man, it's the time I spend with him that counts, not the time I'm not with him. I can forgive long hours or frequent trips if the time we spend together is worthwhile."

"Maybe she wasn't as self-sufficient as you are," Ten suggested.

"Do you know whom she cheated on you with?"

"I didn't want to know," Ten said bluntly. He was

not making this up. So far the only thing he'd lied to Lana about was his real last name, occupation and current place of residence. However, his lies were for the purposes of his assignment only. Everything else he shared with Lana was the truth. Monica, whom he'd dated for over a year, had admitted cheating on him after he returned from an assignment that had kept him away from her for six weeks. To him that had not been a long time. But to a woman who was used to having men fall at her feet, it was an eternity. He hadn't been able to contact her due to the clandestine nature of the assignment and she was livid. She said she'd cheated to teach him a lesson and that no one ignored Monica. Lesson learned.

"I learned that I can't keep a woman based solely on my good looks and charm," he said to Lana with a slight smile on his face. "I obviously didn't give her what she needed."

Lana smiled back at him and patted his hand consolingly. "What you needed was a different woman. I've known you all of twenty-four hours and here we are having breakfast together after sleeping together. Okay, we didn't *sleep* together but you get my drift." She playfully giggled. "You're a catch. So what if you have a demanding job that keeps you on the road a lot. There is a woman out there who'll appreciate you, even thrive on you. She just wasn't the one."

Are you the one? Ten found himself wondering. Once again he had to shake loose those annoying emotions that kept coming to the surface when he was around Lana.

"If you say so," he said noncommittally. He smiled again as he stood up and collected their plates. "You want to wash or dry?"

Lana stood up, too, and began clearing the rest of the dishes from the table. "No, no, you cooked, I'll do the dishes. Go home already. I've kept you long enough. I'm sure that burglar is long gone, probably planning his next heist."

"I'd hate to leave you alone," Ten reluctantly said. He did, however, have something to do that required privacy. To pull it off, he needed to know where Lana and her father would be for the next few hours. Wangling an invitation to go with her to pick up her father would accomplish that. "Besides, imagine how favorable I'll look in your dad's eyes if I'm with you when you pick him up at the hospital. He hasn't exactly agreed to do the documentary yet, you know. I need all the brownie points I can earn."

Lana laughed. "Okay," she happily agreed. He'd been so kind to her. She couldn't get in the way of his scoring her father's permission to invade his life for the next few months, or however long it took to produce a documentary.

"I'll go shower and change and wait for your call," he said as he placed the dishes in the sink and began running hot water. "Then I'll pick you up." He turned the water off, and reached into his jeans pocket and withdrew a battered business card with his cell phone number on it.

Lana accepted it. Looking into his eyes, she said, "All right. I'll see when he's going to be released, and give you a holler."

"You'll have less than an hour to install the bugs," Ten told Pete Baylor, one of the three field agents on his team, over the phone.

"I thought you said…" Pete began.

"I know what I said," Ten said regrettably, "but, before, I was just guessing someone was following her. Now I *know* someone is."

"That private detective you tailed name's Terrick Simpson. He's an ex-cop," Pete reported. "Recently set up shop, and he seems to be a decent enough guy."

"Did you find out who hired him to confirm Lana's arrival?"

"Nah," answered Pete. "I checked out his office myself late last night after he'd gone home. Getting into his computer was pretty easy. There was a sizable cash payment made last week. Next to it he wrote, Client X. Apparently, Client X doesn't want to be identified."

"Okay," Ten said, "so it appears that his assignment was to verify that Lana is back in town. He saw her at the airport in Norfolk, and then followed her to the hospital in Kitty Hawk and took a few photos. But after leaving the hospital he went back to the office. Whoever hired him doesn't want him to keep tabs on her."

"That would be my guess," Pete confirmed.

"Then, last night, someone broke into Lana's father's house and riffled through the drawer where she usually keeps her jewelry, found nothing and was chased out of the house by the family dog."

Pete laughed. "Ferocious, huh?"

"Nah, he's a sweetheart," Ten told him. "I've got to go. Be out of the house by 12:15."

When Ten got over to the Braithwaite house, Lana was on the beach adjacent to the house chasing Bowser who'd slipped past her when she'd gone onto the porch to wait for Ten's arrival.

"Come back here, you sneaky little devil," he heard her yell as she ran after the rambunctious Labrador. She was wearing a bright yellow sleeveless sundress.

Her natural hair bounced in thick curls as she ran and her brown skin glowed with vitality. Ten stood and watched her.

She stopped in her tracks and bent to pick up something she'd seen in the sand.

She turned it over in her hand. Whatever it was, its surface glinted golden in the bright sunlight. From his vantage point, Ten thought it might be a piece of jewelry.

When he reached her side he saw that he'd been right. It was a man's watch, a very expensive one.

Lana looked up at him and he saw that finding the watch had unnerved her. She held it out to him. "This belongs to my husband," she said tensely.

Ten reached for it and she gave it to him. He turned it over, looking for an engraving. There was none. "How can you be sure?"

Lana moved close and pointed to a small nick into the gold underneath the watch's face. When the watch was being worn it would be unnoticeable. But off the wrist you could clearly see it. "That was made," she told him, "according to Jeremy, by the blade of a knife wielded by a mugger who tried to take the watch from him. This watch was the first luxury item Jeremy bought when he had begun to get rich. He was not going to give it up without a fight. Stupid decision, because he got cut that night. Or that's how he told me he got the scar on his wrist and the nick in his beloved Rolex. But that's probably just another lie."

With that she turned, and began walking back toward the house. Bowser had tired of his little game and walked alongside her, ready to take his punishment. Lana was in no mood to mete out punishment to the exuberant dog, though. She just felt unbearably sad. All her fears had been realized. Jeremy's watch wouldn't have been on this beach if Jeremy wasn't close by. The burglar last night had to have been Jeremy, entering her father's house to retrieve something valuable he'd left there on one of his visits there with her. And she was going to figure out just what that was.

Woodenly, she walked onto the porch with Bowser in tow, and locked him inside the house. Walking back down the steps, she said to Ten who was waiting there with the watch, "Jeremy was here last night. He obviously copied the key to the house Dad had given me. He probably used a Jet Ski to reach the beach last night, and had a boat waiting a few yards off shore. That's why I didn't hear a car. He's alive and well and he wants something that I have. The problem is…I don't know what it is."

She reached for the watch, and he gave it to her with reluctance. He wished he could think of an excuse to hold on to it for a while. He'd like to have it dusted for fingerprints. What if this watch belonged to some other rich idiot who'd lost it on the beach?

His gut, however, told him she was right—and his hunch had been right, as well. Now all they had to do was set a trap for the rat-bastard.

"What do you want to do, call the police and tell them you suspect the burglar is Jeremy?"

Lana shook her head. "No, I want to catch him myself."

Ten opened the car door for her. "That could be dangerous," he warned her.

"Oh, he doesn't want to kill me," Lana said confidently. "If he'd wanted to hurt me he could have done it last night. He needs me. I've just got to beat him at his own game. He's looking for something. I've got to find it before he does."

Ten saw the calculating gleam in her eye and knew, no matter what he said, she was determined to have her way. She climbed into the car, and he shut her door and jogged around to the driver's side. Once he was behind the wheel, he turned to her. "What can I do to help?"

She gave him the most brilliant smile he'd ever seen since they met. "I'm not done figuring out my next move," she told him. "But I'm sure I can come up with something you can do to help bring him down."

Ten smiled. He liked the steely tone of her voice. This was a woman with a purpose—to nail her lying, thieving husband to the wall.

He liked her more and more.

Her strength and resilience in the face of great odds made him feel guilty for having to deceive her. She had already been devastated by her husband's deception. He reminded himself that he was only doing his job. When this was over, she would understand that his actions had been dictated by the need to apprehend a fugitive.

Still, he couldn't shake the strong desire to somehow be the hero that she deserved.

Officer Edwards was in Aaron's hospital room discussing the break-in when Lana and Ten arrived. Lana went right in, and kissed her father's cheek.

"Officer Edwards," she said in greeting.

"Mrs. Corday," he acknowledged with a nod. "Your father was telling me it's been a long time since he changed the security code at his house. I suggested he get in the habit of changing it periodically."

"Good advice," she agreed wholeheartedly.

Ten and Officer Edwards nodded at each other without a word passing between them. "How are you, sir?" Ten asked Aaron.

Aaron was already dressed and ready to roll. He couldn't wait to blow this joint. He explained that the hospital staff had tried to feed him breakfast earlier but he'd refused to eat another tasteless meal. But his stomach was growling now because of it. "I'll feel a hundred percent better once I'm home," he said.

"Then let's go," Lana said cheerily. She regarded Officer Edwards. "That is if you're finished with my father."

"Yeah," he said. "Thank you for your time, Mr. Braithwaite."

"Thank you, Officer," Aaron said with a smile.

In Officer Edwards's absence, Lana let out a long breath, and said, "Good, he's gone. Daddy, I've got something to tell you but I think it's best if we wait until we're in the car. Let's get out of here."

Aaron's curiosity was instantly piqued. Her excitement was contagious. Something had happened to buoy her spirits between now and the break-in at the house. His gaze traveled to Ten. Ten's placid expression gave him no clues as to what that might be.

Before they could make their escape, however, a nurse, moving as if she were on speed, strode in pushing a wheelchair. "Here we are, Mr. Braithwaite. If you'll sit down, I'll escort you out."

She picked up a large plastic bag with a cloth drawstring that had the hospital's logo on it and put it in Aaron's lap after he sat down.

Lana and Ten followed the nurse as she pushed Aaron to the elevator. Aaron looked up at Lana and rolled his eyes. He was definitely not enjoying this. He was polite to the nurse, though. Lana had never known him to be rude to someone who was just doing her job. When they got outside into the bright sunshine and the nurse retreated back into the building with the wheelchair, Aaron took the bag, which contained no personal effects and threw it into a nearby trash receptacle.

"It's not as if I'm ever going to use this stuff again," he mumbled.

Lana laughed. She went and put her arm about his shoulders as they stood there waiting for Ten to bring the car around.

In the car on the way home, Lana told Aaron who she suspected the burglar was. Something else had occurred to her, too. "Jeremy probably saw you set the alarm several times over the years. His con-artist brain is like a steel trap. He wouldn't forget something like that," she said aloud.

Lana sat in the back while her dad rode shotgun. "I told Officer Edwards I couldn't think of anyone who would know the code besides the security firm personnel," Aaron said.

"That's good," Lana said, "because I don't want the police involved in this right now. Their presence would scare him off, and I want him to feel confident that no one suspects the truth."

"Now wait a minute, Lana Jo…" Aaron began.

"Lana Jo?" said Ten.

"My middle name's Josephine after my grand-mother," Lana told him. "And I don't want to hear any jokes about it." She met his eyes in the rearview mirror, but hers were smiling regardless of the rigid tone in her voice.

Ten laughed. "Hey, I don't have a leg to stand on with a middle name like Magnus."

Lana guffawed. "Magnus! Your parents really *were* running out of ideas when they named you."

Aaron laughed, too. "Can we get back to the subject? Lana Jo, you're not thinking of trying to catch Jeremy on your own, are you?"

"Yes," Lana said without hesitation. "I'm going to trap him, hogtie him and hand him over to the FBI. You can't tell me he doesn't have it coming."

"Oh, he has it coming, all right," her dad said, "but you're not the one who should be dishing it out. The man's obviously desperate. Why else would he risk capture by breaking into my house and going after whatever he was after? His getaway cash is running low. Don't think that because you were married to him he won't turn on you violently to get what he's after. No, I forbid your getting involved. Call the FBI, and tell them what you know. Don't you agree, Ten?"

Ten was in an untenable position. This case was progressing in a haphazard manner. He felt as if he were losing control of it. Lana was behaving irrationally, almost high on the notion of giving her husband some payback. Also, it appeared that Aaron was on the brink of revealing his identity. And his was the worst point, because at that moment Ten wanted to tell Lana who he really was and that if they all remained calm they could work together to bring Jeremy to justice. If he did that he'd be going against the rules because he was supposed to get permission before blowing his cover.

Ten noticed that it was only eleven forty-five. The team had been told they had until twelve-fifteen. "Why don't we stop for lunch and discuss it?" he suggested.

Aaron was all for that. "There's a steakhouse on the right."

"As long as you restrict yourself to the salad bar," Lana put in.

"My doctor said no butter or lobster," Aaron defended himself. "He didn't say anything about filet mignon."

"In your dreams," Lana countered.

"I'm turning in," Ten said as he steered the car into the steakhouse's parking lot.

Before long they'd been seated, and Aaron had begun to devour a small flank steak and a big salad. Lana had ordered the roast chicken and Ten had the T-bone, which Aaron kept looking at as if he coveted it. "It's dry," Ten told him, steadily slicing into the juicy steak and chomping on it with strong, white teeth.

"Yeah, you're eating it like it's just awful," Aaron said sarcastically.

Lana watched both men with a smile on her face. It was obvious that her dad liked Ten. The two of them shared an easy repartee, often one-upping each other. Which made her wonder why earlier Ten had expressed a fear that her dad would not allow him to do the documentary. It seemed to her that it was a done deal.

"Back to our discussion," she said as she put down her fork. She looked into her father's eyes. "I feel empowered for the first time in a long time. Let me get him, Daddy. I want him to know he didn't break me."

"When the FBI has him in custody, you can visit him in jail and let him know that" was Aaron's only reply.

Ten put down his fork, too, and regarded both of them from his side of the table. "I'm probably going to get fired for doing this, but you two are the most infuriating people I've ever met." He paused. "Lana, you're already involved in a scheme to capture Jeremy. I'm with the FBI, and your father went into the hospital for tests in order to lure you back home. I'm sorry we had to resort to this but even though we've been able to track down some of the funds Jeremy stole, there is still over two hundred million unaccounted for."

Aaron picked up his fork again, and continued eating. "I'd better finish this since it's probably going to be my last meal."

He looked Lana in the eye. She was furious.

Chapter 6

Lana regarded Ten, her expression implacable. She held out her hand, palm up. "Give me your keys."

"I'm not…"

"Keys!" she demanded, not raising her voice but not backing down, either.

Ten gave her the keys.

She palmed them, then gave her father and Ten a sweeping look of disgust. "I'm going for a drive. I might just drive to the airport and catch the first flight heading west. You two can find another way home."

She spun on her heels and marched out of the restaurant. Ten got up to follow, but Aaron reached up and pulled him back down. "Give her some space, son. She's got a temper like her mother. When that woman was on the warpath, I took cover. She didn't get mad often but when she did there was hell to pay." With that said, he continued eating. "You know, this flank steak isn't half bad."

Ten took his cell phone out, and dialed Pete Baylor's number. He had to make sure Pete and the other agents were out of the Braithwaite house. He doubted Lana would go directly home but he couldn't take the chance.

"No problem," said Pete. "We're clear and heading back to the van."

Ten hung up, and continued eating his meal.

"I should be feeling some remorse for taking part in this right about now, I'm sure," said Aaron as he speared some spinach salad with his fork, "but I don't. Lana Jo's back. You can't imagine how worried I was about her. For months she didn't even sound like herself on the phone. The life had gone out of her. She's got her spark back. And I have you and the FBI to thank for it."

"Save your thanks for later," Ten said. "I don't know if this operation can be salvaged or not. I'm holding off phoning my supervisor until I know what Lana plans to do with the information I just gave her."

"You did the right thing," Aaron told him. "We couldn't have Lana acting like an amateur sleuth. She'll come around. Give her a few hours to cool off."

Lana was on Highway 12, the main highway that connected the Outer Banks to the mainland. The SUV handled like a dream, and she had it above the speed limit, heading nowhere in particular. She just wanted to drive and keep on driving.

She should have known Ten was too good to be true. A sensitive filmmaker who loves books? He sounded more like the hero from her favorite romance novel.

Her cell phone rang. She slowed down. She didn't want to wind up a statistic. A quick glance at the display told her it was Grant phoning. Deciding she needed to take his call, she slowed further, and turned into the parking lot of a strip mall. Parked, she answered, "Hello."

"Lana, I've got good news. Your divorce has been granted. They tried to hold it up by insisting that you needed to show proof that you'd made an effort to locate Jeremy but I reminded them who Jeremy is. If the FBI can't find him, what makes them think you can?" He laughed. "Am I right?"

Lana managed to let out a soft laugh. "Thank you, Grant. This is the cherry on top of a truly weird day."

"You sound peculiar, Lana. Is something wrong?"

"I'll explain everything the next time I see you," she promised. "But I do appreciate your help. I'm happy to be the newest ex-wife of Jeremy Corday."

"Are you available tonight?" Grant asked. "I'd like to take you out to dinner to celebrate."

"I'm not in town," Lana told him. "My dad had a health scare, and I'm in North Carolina."

"Oh," said Grant, the concern evident in his tone, "I hope he'll be all right."

"He's going to be fine," Lana assured him. "Thanks for the invitation, though."

Grant was silent for a moment. "Um, okay. I guess I'd better go."

Lana had the distinct feeling that there was more Grant wanted to say. It hadn't escaped her notice over the years that he found her attractive. Maybe since she was now a free agent he wanted to take their relationship to the next level.

She had no intention of encouraging him in that direction. She liked Grant but she knew she could never give his interest the attention it deserved.

"All right," she said, keeping her tone light. "You take care, Grant."

"You, too," he said, before hanging up.

Lana set the phone on the seat, and put the car in Drive again. What she needed was a good long run, not a good long drive. She needed to sweat this mood right out of her body.

When she got back to the house, her father and Ten were already there.

They were in the living room watching a basketball game. Lana tossed Ten his keys as she walked through the living room on the way upstairs to change into her running gear. "Nice ride," she said.

Ten looked up at her hopefully. He opened his mouth to say something.

"I'm still mad at you," she informed him icily, before running upstairs.

"It's not time yet," Aaron advised Ten, then went back to watching the game.

Ten slumped on the couch. "She hates me."

"So? Haven't you ever been hated by a woman before? It's a rite of passage for men. Suck it up!"

Aaron stuffed popcorn in his mouth, and chewed thoughtfully. Lunch hadn't satisfied his hunger. His hospital stay had made him feel as if he were coming off a hunger strike. "Take it this way, son. She wouldn't be so mad at you if she didn't like you. Women don't waste that kind of anger on someone they don't care about."

Ten sat back on the couch and relaxed a bit. Did Lana have feelings for him? His heartbeat quickened at the thought. This was so unlike him. He was normally able to keep his personal life and his work separate, never giving a thought to the desirability of female subjects who were under his protection. Now this hardheaded woman was getting under his skin. He had to man up and take control of this assignment before it all blew up in his face.

Upstairs Lana was fuming. Bowser had abandoned the men and followed her to her bedroom where he sat in the doorway watching as she began pulling off clothes and tossing the pieces onto the bed. "Divorced!" she mumbled. "How am I supposed to feel about that? I'm legally free of a man who obviously didn't want to be with me, anyway.

"Oh, no, wait. He fled because he was going to get sent to prison not because he wanted to get away from *you*. If not for his legal problems, you probably would have spent the next ten years believing you were married to a man who really loved you. Foolish!"

She was wriggling into a sports bra as she continued, "I should be happy I'm rid of him. The world is mine. I can do whatever I want, go wherever I want, *date* whomever I want. Or just entirely give up men—who needs 'em?"

In a van parked on the public side of the beach, Pete was listening in. "Her divorce came through," he announced to his partners, Carrie Jenkins and Eduardo Como. "She's officially off men."

Carrie, a tall blonde with brown eyes, chuckled. "Been there, done that."

"You can do me anytime, Jenkins," said Eduardo, wiggling his thick brows in a seductive manner.

"Bite me, Como," she told him.

"Where?" Eduardo returned.

"Shut up, guys, I'm listening here," Pete said.

In her bedroom, Lana had suited up. She did a couple of leaps in the air to loosen up her calf muscles. She looked down at Bowser. "Wanna go for a run, fella?"

Bowser barked, and followed her downstairs. They made a quick detour to the kitchen for her fanny pack. In the living room she found her dad and Ten exactly

where she'd left them, turning into a couple of egg-
plants in front of the TV.

"I'm going for a run," she announced. She and
Bowser headed for the front door.

"Not without me," Ten said, springing up from the
couch. He was already wearing running shoes and a
track suit. He pulled off his jacket. It was warm outside. The white sleeveless T-shirt he had on under the
jacket would do.

Lana ignored him as she did warm-up exercises
on the porch. Ten followed her example and stretched
along with her. "So, how long have you been running?"
he asked to see if she'd cooled off while she'd been
upstairs.

No such luck. Lana cut him with her eyes. "Practically all my life," she said coldly. With her eyes nar-
rowing further, she asked, "Was anything you told
me the truth?"

"Everything I told you was the truth except my
name's Isles, not West. I'm not a filmmaker and I don't
live in D.C. I live in San Francisco."

"Agent Tennison Isles from the San Francisco field
office," Lana said derisively. "You've probably been
on Jeremy's case from the beginning. Why is it I've
never met you? I've met several other agents from that
office."

"I supervise my team. I chose to remain unknown to
you until now and I'm here because this was my idea,
and my supervisor told me to run with it."

Ten knew that off in the van, Pete would be listening but he didn't care.

They'd worked with Ten on a number of assignments and he'd been all business. Ten was sure they called him a tight-ass behind his back. A former marine, he had more discipline in his little finger than they had in their entire bodies put together. Now they would see that he had an Achilles' heel. And her name was Lana Corday.

On the porch, Lana was doing calf stretches. "So it was your idea to get my father involved?"

"We thought he'd be more willing than you would be," Ten told her frankly.

She laughed shortly. "Well you pegged him right. He never liked Jeremy."

"What father doesn't have a problem with the man his daughter marries?"

Lana shot him an irritated look. "Jeremy got the jump on you that first night, didn't he? You didn't suspect he was that close."

"You're right," Ten admitted, "and I'm sorry about that."

Lana breathed deeply and let it out. It struck her how close she had been to getting seriously hurt. If Jeremy were more ruthless he might have tortured her until she gave him what he'd come for instead of running away once he was discovered.

"This case isn't turning out the way you planned," she deduced.

"That's an understatement," Ten admitted.

Finished stretching, Lana ran down the front steps. Bowser ran ahead of her, leading the way down the beach toward the Easterbrook house. "I'd like some alone time," Lana tossed over her shoulder at Ten. She just wanted to grieve her lost marriage in her own way.

"I can't let you do that, Lana." He stubbornly jogged alongside her.

"You can't keep up with me," she said, her tone deadly serious.

"I'm an ex-marine. I can run you into the ground," Ten warned.

"Okay, Mr. T-bone steak," Lana said with a smirk. She had barely had the chance to get started on her roast chicken before Ten had spoiled her appetite by confessing who he really was. On the other hand, he'd probably eaten that entire steak after she'd disappeared with his car. He was a man wasn't he?

One thing a runner knew was that you didn't run on a full stomach. Not any great distance, anyway. She was going to run *him* into the ground.

So they ran.

During the first mile, talking to each other was no problem. Lana told him about the Outer Banks and why due to the manner in which the barrier islands jutted out into the Atlantic Ocean, that the area was prone to violent storms.

As they picked up pace along the oceanside, Lana looked out into the water. "Many ships had gone down in the Outer Banks, many lives lost. Of course that kind of history can brew some juicy ghost stories about pirates and hapless sailors and fishermen. Dad used to tell me one when I was kid about Blackbeard's ghost. He would hide from the authorities near here in a place called Ocracoke Island. He died near there. Ocracoke's still around. Dad said on stormy nights you could see Blackbeard's ship fighting the waves and him aboard, defying God and daring the lightning to strike him." She laughed as she ran. "I used to dream I was on that ship with Blackbeard and he would chase me all over it, trying to slice me up with his hook. I know, I know, I was mixing him up with Captain Hook from *Peter Pan* but I was just a kid."

By the fifth mile Ten could no longer carry on a conversation. In fact, he felt as if his lunch was about to reappear. Bowser had called it quits after mile two, whined and turned back toward home. Ten wished he were as sensible as the dog. Lana fairly glowed with energy. She was sweating just as he was. She wasn't a superwoman. But she looked as if she could run another ten miles with little effort.

"Tell the truth," he gasped. "You've been training for a marathon."

"Nah," she said. "But I have been putting in an average of about fifty miles a week lately. It's that bastard, Jeremy. I run more when I'm upset."

"And I upset you today," Ten concluded. "I'm sorry, and so are my lungs."

He stopped abruptly, bent over and threw up.

Lana ran in place for a while, then gave it up and tried to approach him to offer help but he held out his hand, keeping her at a distance. There was no pretty way to vomit. And he didn't want her sympathy at that moment.

Lana felt terrible. She'd pushed him on purpose just to prove her point—you shouldn't eat a big meal and run afterward.

Lana always carried water in her fanny pack when she ran. She opened the bottle, and handed it to Ten once he'd finished heaving.

"I'm sorry," she said softly and sincerely.

Ten gratefully accepted the water bottle, took a swig, swished it around in his mouth, and then spit it out. He looked at her and smiled weakly. "It's my fault for being such a competitive jerk. I didn't want to admit you're a better athlete than I am." He kicked sand over the vomit, after which they began walking back in the direction of the house.

"Maybe I'm a better runner," Lana allowed, "but I bet you can kick my butt with that ex-marine martial arts stuff you must know."

"Oh, sure," Ten groaned, "like I'm going to beat up a lady."

Lana laughed delightedly. The sight and sound made Ten feel better. "Does this mean you've forgiven me after watching me puke my guts out?"

"That's a possibility," Lana said noncommittally.

When they got back to the house, Ten reached out and grabbed Lana's arm before she took a step onto the front porch. "Lana, there's one more thing. While we were picking up your father at the hospital my team planted listening devices in the house."

Lana's eyes held a startled look. "My bedroom, too?" she croaked.

"Yes," he said. "Sorry, but it's a means of keeping you safe. If I'd had it done earlier, we would've been there for you when Jeremy broke in."

"Then you're the last of your team to find out I'm divorced. My lawyer phoned after I borrowed your car. I was upset and was talking to myself—I *thought*—while I changed into my running clothes. Now I know I wasn't the only person in the room."

"I'm sorry," Ten said again, gazing into her up-turned face. "So I wasn't the only one who upset you."

For Lana, Ten's revelation had paled in comparison to the emotional impact the knowledge that her marriage, something she had believed in with all her heart in the beginning had ended so messily. She didn't even get the chance to face Jeremy over a negotiation table in a lawyer's office. There was no closure to be had, just his capture, which would have to be closure enough.

"Stop apologizing," she said, forcing herself to smile. "You're just doing your job."

"Just one more sorry," Ten said with sincerity. "I'm sorry your marriage had to end the way it did."

"Thanks, Ten," Lana said, genuinely moved. She stood smiling up at him for a few moments. Then she unlocked the door, and they went inside. "Daddy, we're back!"

Aaron was nowhere to be seen. Lana found a note on the kitchen counter: *Your old English teacher says I've been a bad boy and deserve to be punished. Don't wait up for me.*

Lana checked the time. It was two forty-five. She handed the note to Ten. "Three hours out of the hospital and he has a date!"

Ten laughed. "Go, Aaron."

Lana laughed, too, then sighed and leaned against the counter. She met Ten's eyes. "There's something else we need to talk about. I still think we have a chance of catching Jeremy."

"Yes, we can still catch him," Ten agreed. "We'd like you to cooperate with us, Lana, but you can't go all gung ho on us and act without thinking. You will wind up getting hurt."

She lowered her gaze, her expression contrite. "For a while there I did get a high off the thought of getting revenge. I apologize for my behavior. I'm willing to follow orders now—whatever it takes to bring him down." She met his gaze again. "I do have a suggestion, though—something you all might not have thought of because you don't know him as well as I do."

"I'm listening," Ten encouraged her.

"Jeremy's a methodical man. Think about how

he broke in here without my being aware of it until Bowser woke me. There I was in a pitch-black room with him while he searched the room obviously using night-vision glasses because how else would he have been able to see in the dark? He's cagey. It takes a lot of smarts and calculation to cheat investors out of half a billion dollars. He thinks carefully before he makes a move. Honestly, the only time I've ever seen him lose his cool was when another man showed me too much attention in his presence. He's gets very aggressive. He has to let the other guy know he's encroaching on his territory and he doesn't like his territory being encroached upon."

"Are you saying you want me to publicly romance you in order to flush him out?"

"That's what I'm saying," she boldly stated. With that she went to the refrigerator and withdrew a couple bottles of spring water. She handed one to Ten. "Give it some thought, and let me know if it's a go. I've got to take a shower."

Ten watched her flounce out of the room, her butt a work of art in those tight shorts, her long legs exquisitely shaped. This case was getting more interesting by the hour.

Chapter 7

Jeremy was staying at a place called the Buccaneer Motel. It wasn't the Hilton. He no longer had Hilton money. But it was clean. The suite he was in came with a kitchenette, which was good because he didn't go out to eat much and he did his shopping late at night. His mode of transportation these days was a nondescript sedan he'd paid cash for that had more rust on it than paint. He'd blown a pile of money renting a boat and a Jet Ski the other night. But that all paled in comparison to the amount of money he'd had to shell out for the private detective. Luckily, the detective still owed him several hours of surveillance work.

He'd been waiting for Lana for more than seven months. What had kept her so long? She was critical to the success of his plans. He figured she would immediately run into her father's arms after such an emotional blow. After he'd sabotaged the yacht and disappeared he had spent a few days at a loyal friend's cabin in the Northern California woods. Then he'd driven to the Outer Banks in a used car he'd paid cash for. A fugitive couldn't expect unlimited help from a friend even if they'd known each other since they were both juvenile delinquents. The friend had gone straight and couldn't risk the life he'd made with his wife and children for the likes of *him*. The loan of the cabin had been the extent of his friend's generosity. The good news was Jeremy wouldn't need anyone's help if he could get his hand on a certain item. With it, he would have access to two hundred and fifty million dollars. It was in the form of diamonds. The unique and wonderful thing about quality diamonds was that their intrinsic value remained stable, unlike cash. But you couldn't use diamonds like currency. Jeremy already had a German buyer who was going to compensate him fifty percent of their worth, once he got hold of them. He would lose quite a bit of money but still he would be able to live the rest of his life on one hundred and twenty-five million.

He was lying in bed now with the TV turned up loud in an attempt to block out his thoughts. Lana. He'd stood there gazing at her after he'd broken into Aaron's house and headed up to her room. Then he'd forced himself to get on with the search for what he'd come for. After searching the room, with no results, he had gone back to look at her one last time. He'd wanted to touch her. Standing so close to her warm body had given him sexual thoughts. She always had that effect on him whenever they were near a bed. He'd wanted to climb into bed with her and make love. But suddenly the dog had woken, and started growling causing Lana to stir in her sleep, and she accidentally touched him. An electric charge swept through him. The dog snapped at his leg and got a mouthful of trouser instead. Still, he lingered a moment longer, looking longingly at Lana who cowered on the other side of the bed, afraid of being attacked by an unknown assailant. He wanted to tell her he'd never hurt her. But self-preservation made him run.

Worst of all, as he was being chased from the room by the mutt, out of the corner of his eye he'd spied the object he'd been looking for on the nightstand. Of course, she'd taken it off before bed as she'd done every night since he'd given it to her on their fifth anniversary.

In spite of his failure to retrieve the locket, something inside of him exulted. She was still wearing it. Maybe that meant she hadn't given up on him. Maybe it meant she still loved him.

He got up now and went to stand in front of the bureau's mirror. He'd lost a few pounds but his body still had the well-defined musculature of a runner. It was one of the things he and Lana had liked doing together. He was still movie-star handsome. Golden skin, curly blond hair, blue eyes, strong square-chinned face and dimples. Women often said that he reminded them of that Australian actor, Hugh somebody. Only his hair was much lighter in comparison to the dark-haired actor.

He remembered the first time he'd seen Lana. She was a guest at a party at the home of clients who wanted to show off their newly decorated home. The couple, who was extremely rich, was also on his radar as potential investors. That night, after spotting Lana, he had forgotten all about his bank account and concentrated on getting her number. She was wearing a little black dress with sexy high-heeled sandals. Her legs were killer, as was every curve of her brown-skinned body. Her natural red hair fell in waves down her back. He'd walked over to her, knowing he was probably the best-looking male in the room, and said, "I would die happy if for one second I could be that dress you're wearing."

He'd instantly known that no man had ever said anything so bold to her before. She looked at him in amazement. Then she'd laughed, and said, "What's your name?"

He looked himself dead in the eye in the mirror and smiled. "Soon, Lana, you're going to be calling my name in the throes of passion like you used to."

He turned away from the mirror, and began pacing the room. First he had to figure out how to get that locket, because concealed inside it was the key to his future.

* * *

"Catch, boy!" Lana yelled to Bowser as he leaped into the air to grasp the Frisbee between his jaws. Landing, he twirled around in a crazy dance reminding Lana of the victory dance some football players executed when they made a touchdown.

"He's on fire." Ten laughed at Bowser's antics.

Bowser trotted over to him and placed the Frisbee at his feet. Ten picked it up and sent it sailing high in the air. By the time it was arcing downward Bowser was under it ready to catch it. This time when he caught it, he rolled over with it in his mouth, sand covering his fur. Lana laughed. He was such a ham.

It was Saturday afternoon, two days after their run. Ten and Lana were playing with Bowser on the beach several yards from the house while Aaron and his lady friend, Lana's former English teacher, Miss Ellen Newman, were grilling seafood on the back deck. Miss Newman, as it turned out, was a good influence on Aaron. Lana was having a hard time not thinking of her as Miss Newman, even though she'd asked her to call her Ellen. It was also kind of weird seeing the suggestive looks passing between Miss Newman and her dad. Not that she assumed her father didn't have a love life. She knew he did. She just felt uncomfortable knowing anything about it. Don't ask, don't tell was fine with her when it came to his affairs.

Anyway, she thought, *why am I wasting time thinking about my dad's love life when I could be looking at that?* Tennison Isles, special agent with the FBI, was a vision to behold in his swim trunks. He was all man. Broad, muscular chest, six-pack, biceps for days, and the legs, thighs and butt weren't bad, either. He even had nice feet, large and perfectly suited to his big frame. She sighed. She had to force herself not to ogle the poor guy who, she was sure, didn't think of her in that way. To him she was just a means to an end. He was there to see the assignment through and try to keep her safe at the same time.

He'd told her this morning that he'd spoken to his supervisor, and the FBI was grateful to her for agreeing to help them capture Jeremy. They'd given him the go-ahead to pose as her love interest if it would help them reach their goal faster.

They were to spend as much time together as possible and be seen in and around town enjoying themselves. Tonight they were going to the anniversary party of Bobbi Lee and her husband, Ronald, which was to be held at a popular restaurant in nearby Kitty Hawk.

"Soup's on!" yelled Aaron.

Ten was rubbing sand onto the Frisbee in order to get the dog spit off of it.

Bowser was watching with the hope that the human would throw the darn thing again. He still had plenty of energy left.

Lana said, "Let's go eat. I'm starved."

Bowser forgot about the Frisbee at the mention of

the word *eat*. It was one of his favorites, right up there with *play*. He raced ahead of them as Lana and Ten began walking to the house.

There was a breeze off the ocean, and seagulls flew above the foamy caps that the wind whipped up. The blue sky was crystalline. Ten looked at Lana whose hair was blowing in the breeze and realized that it had been a long time since he'd spent a more idyllic day. Earlier they'd gone for a swim and she was like a sleek seal in the depths, comfortable with the waves as they fought against them. He supposed living out here she had probably learned to swim as a toddler. It was like her natural element.

Before sitting down to eat, Lana and Ten changed clothes, and Bowser had to be cleaned up too after his triumphant roll in the sand.

Aaron put on some classic soul. While they feasted on grilled shrimp and salmon with garden salad, grilled eggplant, and corn on the cob, they listened to Otis Redding, Al Green, Gladys Knight and the Pips, Marvin Gaye and The Spinners.

Lana and Aaron hadn't told Ellen who Ten really was. Because other people in town like Miss Gladys and her husband, Henry, knew him as the filmmaker who was doing a documentary on Aaron, that remained his cover. She was also told that he was Lana's new boyfriend. That information, to Lana's dismay, made Ellen want to talk Lana up, and in a fit of nostalgia she started recalling Lana's high school days. She had a good memory.

"Lana was one busy young lady her senior year in high school," Ellen told Ten. Ellen was in her early fifties but looked like she was in her forties thanks to a healthy lifestyle. She had smooth dark brown skin with red undertones, brown eyes, and wore her black hair in a short, layered cut that accentuated her heart-shaped face.

She scrunched up her pretty face now as she seemingly had difficulty recalling exactly how busy Lana had been. "Let's see, she was a cheerleader, was on the track team, was vice-president of the senior class; and what else…oh, yes, she was on the homecoming court."

Lana blushed. "I hated being bored."

"I was in ROTC in high school," Ten said. "That's about it."

"Always meant for the military, huh?" Aaron chimed in as he bit into a juicy shrimp.

Lana gave him the evil eye.

"I'm cutting down," he said. "See? I only have a couple on my plate."

"Yeah," Ten answered Aaron's question, smiling. "It runs in my family. My dad was an army man, two of my brothers are marines, as I was, and two of my other brothers were in the army also. I have a sister who is also a marine. When they retire from the military they go into law enforcement."

"Really," said Ellen. "They must have been surprised when you chose to become a filmmaker after you left the service."

"As a matter of fact, they still think I'll eventually come around and become a policeman."

Lana lightly kicked him underneath the table. The amused gleam in her eye told him she knew he was having fun at Ellen's expense.

"Maybe they're even hoping you might one day join the CIA or the FBI," she said.

Now Ten *knew* that Lana was enjoying the performance as well.

"Oh, I could never be a part of either one of those agencies," Ten said. "Too much subterfuge and I hear they have to do reprehensible things in the service of their country, like kill somebody." He gave her a pointed look.

Lana swallowed hard as if she were sure he meant her.

Ten nearly laughed but contained it. "I'm more comfortable with books, not guns."

Ellen looked at him with admiration. "That's my area of expertise. Tell me, just off the top of your head, what's your favorite book of all time?"

Ten smiled in Aaron's direction. "The best writer in America today is sitting right here at this table."

Aaron laughed as if what Ten had said were ludicrous. He cleared his throat and took a sip of his iced tea before saying, "You have my permission to name your favorite book besides my masterpieces," he said.

"Well, then, *Invisible Man* by Ralph Ellison," Ten said without hesitation. "I think the theme of racial invisibility is still relevant today."

"Yeah," Aaron agreed, "but for sheer power you can't beat Richard Wright's characterization of Bigger Thomas in *Native Son*. He's a character I've never forgotten.

"And if I'm correct Richard Wright was one of Ralph Ellison's mentors."

"Bigger Thomas *is* a memorable character," Ellen said softly. "But my most memorable character is Janie in *Their Eyes Were Watching God* by Zora Neale Hurston. Before Maya Angelou ever wrote that 'Phenomenal Woman' poem, Janie was a phenomenal woman."

"I totally agree with that," Lana said, smiling at Ellen.

"You've read it, Lana?" asked Ellen, obviously delighted.

"Yes," Lana told her, "but don't make me write a paper on it. Some of the details are fuzzy after all these years."

Everyone laughed, and the conversation turned to music. Otis Redding's "These Arms of Mine" began playing, and Aaron stood up and asked Ellen to dance right there on the deck.

She happily got up, and they began slowly swaying to the romantic song.

Aaron shot Ten an irritated look. "Get up and dance

with my daughter, son. Life's too short to let an opportunity pass you by."

Ten was more than happy to oblige. Lana looked up into his eyes, and grasped his hand. "Don't let him bully you," she whispered as he pulled her close against his chest.

"Darling," Ten said softly in her ear, "You're way too tense. Relax. I'm enjoying being your *suitor*."

"Boyfriend," she corrected him. "Suitor sounds so old-fashioned."

"Lover?" he said hopefully.

"We haven't gotten that close yet," she countered.

"But soon," he said.

"If you're a good boy," she said, smiling up at him.

"But not too good," he returned.

Lana blushed to the tips of her ears. He was a good dancer. He didn't hold her too tightly and didn't step on her toes once. "For a big man you're not bad," she complimented him.

"I'm good at quite a few things," he said with an enigmatic smile.

Lana felt it was in her best interest to change the subject. She was getting entirely too warm and it clearly wasn't from the temperature, which had begun to lower with the impending sunset.

"Did you all find any prints on the watch?" she asked. She'd given it to him yesterday to see if he could verify her suspicion that the watch belonged to Jeremy.

"No results yet," he said. "Probably by tomorrow."

Lana glanced in her father's direction. He'd led Ellen to the far side of the deck where he was saying something in her ear that made her laugh.

"I've been thinking," Lana said softly. "Jeremy waited until I got here to break into the house therefore what he wants has to be something I must have brought with me. Not something he might have hidden here during a past visit as I had first assumed. It must be something he *knew* I would bring with me from San Francisco."

Her eyes were brilliant, alive with banked excitement as she looked into his. She stopped moving, and touched the locket around her neck. "He gave me this. I wear it everywhere. Could there be something inside of it besides the pictures that I'm aware of?"

"Let me see it," said Ten, stepping backward. He waited while she unfastened the clasp and placed it in his hand. The locket was gold and had an intricately carved image of a weeping willow on its face. When he opened it, on opposite sides of the hinge were photos of people he assumed were Lana's parents. The one of her mother was obviously old and had a sepia tone. The shot of her father had been taken more recently. Ten turned the locket over in his big hands. Looking closely at how it was made. It was shaped like an egg. And it was heavier than he imagined it should be. Maybe it held a a hidden compartment.

"Do you mind if I take it with me?" he asked Lana

who was looking at him with a curious expression on her face.

"Not at all," she said.

"It's getting late," Ten said. "I should go shower and get ready for the party. It starts at eight, right?"

"Yes and wear something sexy," Lana joked. "I want to show you off to my old classmates."

Ten gave her a sharp salute as he bounded down the back steps. "I'll try my best."

Lana watched him go with a smile on her lips.

The place's parking lot was packed. Music was blaring and the huge outdoor dining room was decorated with festive colored lights. Ten got out of his SUV and immediately went over to the passenger's side to open the door for Lana, who was dressed in a beautiful white halter dress. Hand in hand they made their way toward the entrance.

As soon as Lana and Ten entered the reserved dining room of the bar and grill where the anniversary party was being held, screaming erupted. Bobbi Lee and three other women came barreling toward her.

Bobbi Lee reached her first, and hugged her tightly. "You made it." Cheek to cheek, Bobbi Lee said a quick hello to Ten. Then she took Lana by the hand, and led her over to the waiting threesome.

Lana didn't have to be introduced to Gayle Evans, Anastasia Rojas or Siobhan O'Hara. They'd been on her cheerleading squad in high school. Gayle wore her Afro cut short and was as fit as ever. Anastasia looked close to nine months pregnant. But Siobhan had changed the most. In high school she had been about five-two at the most, now she was five-seven.

Lana hadn't seen Siobhan since their sophomore year more than twelve years ago due to her moving away before junior year. Now she was living in the area again. "Siobhan, you had a growth spurt!" was the first thing out of Lana's mouth.

The women laughed. "Pay up," Gayle said to the other women. "I told you she'd be shocked by Siobhan's appearance."

Siobhan, a brunette in a fitted dark pantsuit, smiled up at Lana. "You know, I've always envied your height."

"Yeah, but I had no idea you could increase your height just by wishing," Lana cracked. "You look fabulous. You all do."

Each of them hugged her in turn. Then Lana introduced them to Ten. "Ladies, this is my boyfriend, Tennison West."

Bobbi Lee, who had already met Ten but hadn't known Lana was seeing him, cried, "Well, all right, then!"

Gayle, Siobhan and Anastasia didn't try to hide their delight. Their eyes sparkled with interest.

Ten had a feeling he was in for an interesting evening.

"Welcome, Tennison," cooed Gayle. Her eyes noticeably took all of him in, from the fitted black designer short-sleeved shirt that showed off his biceps and pectorals to the Levi's that couldn't hide his muscular thighs.

"It's a pleasure," Anastasia said, peering up at him and moving forward to shake his hand while keeping one hand on her distended belly. She licked her luscious red lips and smiled saucily.

"Mr. West," said Siobhan nonchalantly.

Ten thought she would be the exception to the rule and not openly flirt with him as her two girlfriends had done. But she winked at him and made no attempt to conceal the gesture from Lana.

"Enough of that," Lana said, laughing. "We're not in high school anymore." She thought Ten deserved an explanation. "We made a game of flirting with each other's boyfriends in high school, harmless of course."

"I'm married now anyway," Gayle said, pretending to be put out by Lana's admittance.

"I'm married and, as you can see, about to pop," Anastasia joked.

"And I'm engaged," Siobhan added. She held up her hand. On her ring finger was a five-carat diamond solitaire. "See?"

Of course, there was more screaming.

As the evening progressed the sexes naturally separated. The women sat around a large table and caught up with each others' lives and munched on various finger foods and sipped from glasses of champagne, while the men gathered at the back of the room where there was a fifty-inch HDTV tuned to ESPN, ate greasy chicken wings and drank cold beer.

Lana, sitting between Bobbi Lee and Siobhan, wondered when the split had happened. She missed Ten. She looked in his direction. He coincidentally looked up at that moment, and they smiled at each other.

"New love," Bobbi Lee said with a note of longing. "I remember the feeling." Then her mood changed in an instant, and she said perkily, "What I want to hear about are all the celebrities you've worked with in San Francisco. Anybody we'd know?" The women looked at Lana expectantly.

She laughed. "I'm not in Hollywood, I'm in San Francisco. Most of the people I've worked with have been professionals. I've done the occasional job for a star athlete but that's as close as I get to glamour."

Siobhan reached over and grasped Lana's hand, "Look, Lana, I'll be the brave one here and get this out in the open, we've all heard about your troubles. You know us down here. We stick together. We never believed anything they said about you. We know you have a good heart. And we're here for you."

Touched, Lana looked into the individual faces of the four women around the table. "I really appreciate that. I was a little leery about coming home. You know how it is…not wanting to look like a failure."

"Honey, you're not the first woman, or man for that

matter, who trusted someone you shouldn't have," Bobbi Lee told her.

Gayle held up her hand as if she were in class and was eager to answer a question posed by the teacher. "Let me jump in by saying I came home from work one night and found my apartment nearly stripped of every piece of furniture I'd bought with my hard-earned money. Had I been robbed? Well, yeah, but by the man I was living with at the time!"

Everyone laughed. No one expressed sympathy because they knew Gayle wasn't looking for sympathy. She was just sharing her experiences in order to let Lana know she wasn't alone.

Siobhan took a long sip of her champagne before chiming in. "I went through a lot of frogs before I found my Prince Charming. One guy tried to manipulate me into thinking I was nothing without him. Verbal abuse was a daily occurrence in my life. Fortunately I got out before he started hitting me. Yeah, girlfriend, I think we can all come up with examples of what it's like to be mistreated by a man."

"But we can also come up with examples of good men," Bobbi Lee said. She glanced at her husband across the room. "Does it bother me that on our anniversary my man is watching sports with the guys? No, not at all because I know his heart's in the right place. He loves me, works hard and he's a good father. No, we're not living the glamorous life, we're both happy."

Lana leaned over and hugged her. "I don't know why it took me so long to come back home."

"Stubborn," Bobbi Lee said. "You've always been stubborn, Lana Jo."

"I'm working on it," Lana told her, not denying she had a problem. She suddenly had an urgent need to go to the bathroom. She'd drunk too much water tonight. Every time someone offered her an alcoholic drink, and there had been several offers because drinkers didn't like to drink alone, she had held up her bottle of spring water and said, "I'm covered." Twenty-four ounces of water later, she had to find the bathroom and quickly.

"Excuse me," she said, "bathroom break."

"I'll go with you," Bobbi Lee offered.

"No, stay," Lana insisted. "I'll be right back."

In her absence, Gayle said, "Has anyone heard anything lately about her husband's case? I didn't want to ask but I'm curious. Is he really dead, or in hiding?"

"Nobody knows," Siobhan told them. "But they never found a body."

"Poor kid," Bobbi Lee added. "She must not know which way is up."

Anastasia's gaze went to Ten. Her friends followed her line of sight. "I think she's heading in the right direction."

The ladies clinked champagne glasses together in agreement.

Across the room Ten had noticed Lana leave the

dining room. He figured she was going to the restroom. But he couldn't let her out of his eyesight any length of time with Jeremy out there somewhere. So he excused himself and followed her.

Ahead of him, he saw her go into the ladies' room. He leaned against the wall in the corridor to wait for her. A couple of waitresses passed by going to and from the kitchen and perused him with interest. He smiled, and they smiled back and kept going.

Lana came out of the ladies' room and immediately spotted him. She smiled widely. "Hey, boyfriend," she said saucily, "how about a little fresh air?"

Ten was definitely game. He had been enjoying talking to the guys. Even though he liked watching sports as well as the next man, spectator sports took a backseat when he could be looking at Lana.

He pushed away from the wall, and walked toward her. Lana loved the way he moved, smoothly and powerfully, his body fine-tuned and masculine. She felt the pull of his sexual magnetism every time she was in his presence and it bothered her. *He* bothered her. She knew Jeremy didn't deserve her loyalty, yet she still felt like a married woman. Being with Ten made her feel as though she were lusting after another man. Lusting after him and contemplating sinning with him. Not just thinking about doing it, but imagining it in great detail.

Ten's hand was at the base of her spine as they walked through the exit and stepped outside onto a large wooden deck. Other patrons of the bar and grill were sitting around tables enjoying themselves. A juke-box was playing "Let's Just Kiss and Say Goodbye" by the Manhattans. Couples danced on the raised plat-form whose backdrop was the beach.

"I love that song," Lana said, closing her eyes as if to bring back a memory.

Ten escorted her to the dance floor and pulled her into his arms. He knew this was a mistake. She pressed her body close and they began moving in sync. He for-got she was off-limits, that this was only a ruse to get a rise out of her now ex-husband. When she relaxed and laid her head on his chest, he closed his eyes and willed himself not to physically react to the smell of her hair and the feel of her skin. The dress she was wear-ing left her arms and part of her back bare. Her skin felt so silky and warm. She smelled of honeysuckle, fresh, not cloying like some fruity colognes can be. He breathed her in.

Lana's body trembled slightly. Was there any turn-ing back from this? Their first dance on her dad's deck had been nothing like this. This felt like a prelude to lovemaking and not just lovemaking but hot, uncon-trollable, mind-blowing sex.

She tilted her head up and as soon as she met his eyes, she knew that he felt it, too.

He wanted her, wanted her as much as she wanted him. She took a deep breath and let it out. "We're in trouble, aren't we?"

"Oh, yeah," Ten said as his mouth claimed hers, "big trouble."

Lana wrapped her arms around his neck, went up on her toes to compensate for his greater height, and held on. He tasted like life-giving nectar, so sweet. She couldn't get enough. Here was her refuge that she had unknowingly been looking for. Her escape from what her reality had become. If she could stay in his arms like this all night, she could face whatever tomorrow would bring.

Ten knew he should stop. And that was his plan. *Any minute now.* But as they came up for air, she released a breathless sigh and those golden-brown eyes regarded him with such longing, he went in for a second taste. Then the music stopped, thank God, and the rest of the patrons started clapping and cheering outrageously. He and Lana parted to learn they were the center of attention. He grabbed Lana by the hand and they hurried off the raised platform and downstairs to the beach.

She was giggling.

He faced her, let go of her hand, and though it was hard to see the seriousness in the situation at the moment because he hadn't been this happy in a long time, he knew he had to inject a bit of reality.

"I shouldn't have done that."

"You didn't do it alone," she said. She got control of the giggles and with hands on her hips regarded him with clear eyes. "Is there some rule against your getting involved with me?"

"As long as the case is ongoing, yes," Ten told her. "It could compromise how well I do my job."

"So you can *pretend* to be my lover but you can't *be* my lover," Lana concluded.

"That's right," said Ten.

"You've never…" Lana began. She wasn't sure she wanted to know the answer, but she had to ask the question nonetheless. This couldn't be the first time he'd had to watch over a woman he'd found attractive.

"No," was Ten's immediate response. "I never before had a problem avoiding touching, kissing or doing anything else with someone under my protection."

"Oh," said Lana, her tone a bit wistful. Inside, she was smiling. Tennison Isles might actually have the capacity for honesty and loyalty, two things she was looking for in the next man she let into her bed. There it was again, *her bed.* She was certain they would eventually end up in bed together.

"So we won't make love," she said, moving in on him again. "We'll just kiss like horny teenagers in the backseat of a car."

Ten gave up. He grabbed her, and kissed her until they were both out of breath. They were alone except for the sand, sea and the moon above.

Chapter 8

Lana awakened to a very quiet house. Usually, when her dad was in the house, there was music playing either somewhere downstairs or out on the deck. But lately it was the beeps, whistles and whatever other sounds video games made. Her dad was getting hooked on them. Surprisingly, he'd said Ellen had turned him on to them. She swore by them, saying they kept her hand-eye coordination sharp.

Lana sat up in bed, stretching as she did so. She yawned widely. *He must be writing,* she thought. She had no idea when her dad's deadline was for his next book but she was sure he was working on something. He always was. His mysteries sold so well that his agent had recently been able to sell his speculative fiction, too. Because he was known as a mystery writer he had been worried that his readers wouldn't embrace another side of him, but the scary stories he'd penned were beginning to outpace the sales of his mysteries. She was so proud of him.

After showering and getting dressed, she went downstairs to the kitchen to see if her dad had left her any coffee. The smell lingered, but that didn't mean there was any left warming in the carafe.

Yes, there appeared to be a couple cups left. She poured herself a cup just as the phone rang. She didn't bother looking at the caller ID and picked up the call quickly, "Hello!"

"Good morning," said Ten.

"Good morning," she replied huskily.

"How are you?"

"Well rested and ready to have some fun on the water today," she told him. Last night when he'd brought her back home she'd invited him to go out on the Jet Skis with her. Her dad had a new model big enough for three riders. They were ideal not only for sports but for rescuing people who got into trouble on the water. Lifeguards used them for that very purpose.

"Me, too," said Ten. "But I called to tell you the results of the fingerprint test. The prints on the watch do in fact belong to Jeremy."

"I knew it!" Lana cried, trying not to gloat. "I wonder if he knows where he lost it. It's probably getting on his last nerve."

* * *

Jeremy was fuming. His Rolex was missing. It had been with him through it all. It was his lucky charm. He'd won it off a guy in Vegas along with a hundred grand. With that hundred grand he'd started his business and the rest was history.

He wanted it back, and the only place he could have lost it was at the Braithwaite house. Somewhere between the time he'd stepped onto the beach and the time he'd spent looking for the locket, his watch must've slipped from his arm. He'd probably lost it while fending off that crazy dog. He'd noticed it was gone when he was riding the Jet Ski back to the boat. He almost wished it'd been on the beach because if he'd lost it anywhere in the house Lana was going to find it. If she did, suspicions would arise. If she still loved him maybe she wouldn't notify the FBI that he'd broken into her father's house. More than likely, though, when she held in her hand proof positive that he was still alive and had left her high and dry she was going to be pissed off.

From now on he had to be proactive. He could no longer hide out in the motel room all day, venturing out only at night. In order to go outside during daylight hours he would need a disguise. It was time to use that hair color he'd purchased on a whim.

Twenty minutes later he looked at himself in the bathroom mirror. His head looked like someone had smeared shoe polish all over his scalp. His curly hair was brown now. The box had promised highlights but he couldn't see any. Hopefully his new hair color would be enough of a disguise. He had a better chance of not being recognized in a small town in North Carolina than in San Francisco. But with the presence of the internet, news traveled fast and furiously. The world was a smaller place because of it.

After thoroughly washing his hair, he took a good look at himself once more in the mirror. With his new curly brown hair, he actually did look like that Hugh guy. He smiled, revealing beautiful white teeth an orthodontist would be proud of.

He'd celebrate by going out to lunch.

Lana and Ten took turns operating the Jet Ski. It was now Ten's turn to pilot the powerful watercraft. Lana had her arms wrapped around his waist. They were wearing lifejackets and stylish safety glasses to guard against sea spray.

On shore Bowser was going crazy running back and forth, trying to follow the path of the Jet Ski. Occasionally he would run into the surf, barking with abandon, but soon the waves would chase him back to shore.

Lana had the side of her face pressed to Ten's back, enjoying the ride. She tried not to think of Jeremy but he was rarely far from her thoughts. She doubted she would ever stop wondering how she let herself be duped by him. Was love truly blind? She guessed in her case it had been. Or had she been too impressed

by his deceptive achievements? By all appearances he
was a gorgeous, charismatic businessman who had a
penchant for making money. He dealt in securities and
his advice had made his rich clients even richer. *That's
why they flock to me, baby,* he used to say, *because I
know how to keep them in the lap of luxury. And who
doesn't like luxury?*

Lana got used to the big house and expensive cars
and designer clothes. Jeremy had plied her with jewelry that had been confiscated along with the house
and the cars. Did she miss them? No. She had lived
without them before she met Jeremy, and she could
live without them now. She could thank her father for
that attitude. She had been blessed to grow up knowing that you appreciated things more when you worked
hard for them.

Her father was a prime example of that. He'd been
a fisherman like his father before him and his father's
father. Yet he'd turned his love of reading into a love
of writing and built a career for himself.

Material possessions given to her by Jeremy were
not things she had earned. Now that she knew how he'd
gotten them, they felt like cursed objects. She was glad
to be rid of them. But she didn't ever think she would
rid herself of the guilt she felt about having been married to Jeremy and not realizing he was a con artist.
She thought of all those elderly people whose savings
accounts were now bare. She wanted desperately to
find those missing funds Ten had told her about.

* * *

Lana had gone to pick up a few things at the supermarket. Not a long list of items, just fresh bread, milk, eggs and some fruits and vegetables. She felt perfectly safe doing so since field agents would be watching her every move. Ten wouldn't be among them because he was in Norfolk checking on the progress of the agency-approved jeweler who was examining the locket for secret compartments.

She strolled down the aisles, perusing the shelves for anything that looked interesting and that might be good for her dad's health, because half the joy of shopping was discovering new things. Then suddenly she became aware of a man standing beside her. He was dressed casually, wearing jeans and a short-sleeved shirt. On his feet, were well-worn canvas boat shoes. There was something awfully familiar about those comfortable-looking navy blue shoes. Oh, yeah, she'd purchased them herself. They were Jeremy's favorite kicking-around shoes. He'd been wearing them the day he'd taken the yacht out.

Her heart seemed to lurch in her chest as her gaze traveled up the length of his body and settled on his familiar face. She wasn't prepared for the shock to her system that seeing him again dealt her.

He didn't appear at all affected by their reunion. He smiled coolly. "Get hold of yourself, darling. I'd really prefer it if we could have a quiet conversation without attracting too much attention."

He put his hand on her upper arm and directed her down the produce aisle. He casually paused, selected a golden delicious apple and put it in her cart.

Lana could barely catch her breath, let alone scream. She stared at him. He didn't look any worse for the wear. Six-two, with a muscular body, he appeared a little slimmer but not much. But with his hair that shade of brown even she had to do a double take to recognize him. It'd definitely been a good decision on his part.

"Like my new look?" he asked, smiling. "I see you cut your hair. I like it!" He kept his voice low and she suspected he expected her to follow suit.

She had to clear her throat a couple times before she could find her voice. "The new look's working for you," she managed to say.

He seemed pleased by the compliment. His eyes were on her chest, and for a moment Lana thought he was actually looking at her breasts but then she realized he was looking for the locket.

"What happened to the locket I gave you?" he asked tightly.

"What happened to your polite tone?" she returned.

"I don't have time to be polite," he said, his eyes momentarily darting about as if he knew someone was following him. He took her by the hand and led her to an alcove adjacent to the produce department and away from customer traffic. "As you know, I'm a wanted man. Now, let's be honest with one another. I'm aware you know I'm the one who broke into your dad's house. You're smart. I'm sure you know why. So, where's the locket?"

"I took it to a jeweler's to be cleaned," Lana lied.

Jeremy smiled. "You're a terrible liar, always have been."

"You should know," she said, also smiling. She was more confident now, and was determined she wasn't going to be intimidated by him. He needed something *she* had, not vice versa.

Jeremy didn't say a thing. His jaw worked as he ground his teeth, a habit he had when he was furious. After a good ten seconds, he tried another tack. He reached into his shirt pocket and retrieved a photograph. He violently thrust it in her face.

"Who the hell is this, Lana?"

Lana didn't try to hide her surprise. The photo was of her and Ten kissing on the dance floor of the bar and grill last Saturday night. "That's someone I'm seeing," she said softly.

Jeremy's blue eyes narrowed. "I'm dead, and you're dating seven months later. Who is he?"

"It's been eight months, and we both know you're not really dead. It's none of your business who he is. Anyway, I divorced you."

"You did what?" Jeremy shouted.

"My lawyer suggested it," said Lana, beginning to enjoy their conversation. She could see by the veins in his neck that he was angry.

"Grant Robinson?" he asked.

"Yes."

"He's always wanted you!" He'd had the good sense to lower his voice again.

"Has he really?" Lana said calmly. "Well, that's beside the point. He convinced me that it was the only way I could reclaim my life after being abandoned by *you,* and he was right. I'm getting along fine without you."

Jeremy took in a deep breath, and said, "Okay, so you were within your rights to divorce me."

"Damn right I was!"

"Okay, okay, calm down," he cajoled. "I can see that you're angry with me for what I did to you. I can apologize, but I don't think you'd believe me. So, what if we make a deal? You should be compensated for the trouble I've put you through. A no-fault divorce is definitely not going to allow you to live in the manner you've become accustomed to. But if you give me the locket, I'll make sure you'll never have to work again for the rest of your life."

Lana smiled thoughtfully. "Who needs you? I've got the locket. I'm smart, I can figure out why you want it so badly."

"You don't have to figure out anything, darling," Jeremy told her. "Inside of the locket is a safe-deposit-box key. However, it could be the key to any safe-deposit box in the world. Only I know the location. You need me."

"No, you need *me,*" Lana said stubbornly. "I can

wait you out. Your runaway cash can't last much longer. Then you'll be living on the street, if you already aren't."

Jeremy gave a resigned sigh. "All right, Lana, I do need you." He looked deeply in her eyes. "Have you contacted the FBI since you've been here?"

"Oh, do you mean have I told them I found your Rolex on the beach?" Lana said with a smirk.

"You found it," he said, sounding almost defeated.

"Yes, and the answer is no, I haven't phoned the FBI, *yet.*"

"What can I do to insure you never bring them into this?" he asked, giving her his signature pleading look. That look usually got her to acquiesce. But she was a different woman today.

"You can give me the location of the safe-deposit box. We'll meet at the bank, get whatever's inside and split it right there. No more games. We part, you disappear forever, and I retain the lifestyle I'd enjoyed while we were married."

Jeremy actually looked pleased with her stipulations. "My, how you've changed. You used to be so sweet and innocent."

"Being accused of being a liar and a cheat even though I didn't do anything must have had a bad effect on me," she said icily.

"Let's go then," Jeremy said.

Eyes wide, Lana asked, "You mean right now?"

"The bank's here in Kitty Hawk," Jeremy told her.

"I put the package in the safe-deposit box nearly two years ago. Of course, you weren't with me on that trip. I lied and said I had to go out of town on business."

"I have to give it to you, it was clever of you to put the key in the locket," Lana said, remembering the night he'd given her the piece of jewelry and said she should always keep it close to her heart. When in reality what was inside was close to his heart.

"You were always thinking ahead. You were counting on my coming home," Lana said in awe. "But I kept you waiting. Ironic, isn't it? Because of your behavior I was being torn apart in the media, and because I stubbornly refused to allow them to get the best of me, I dug my heels in and wouldn't leave San Francisco."

"I'm curious," said Jeremy, his gaze admiring her body in that cute little sundress she had on. "Why did you finally show up?"

"My dad got sick."

"I'm sorry." His eyes took on a sympathetic look.

Lana hated him more at that instance. He was so adept at feigning emotions.

"Save it, I don't believe a word out of your mouth anymore," she hissed. "I suffered because of you. I couldn't eat. I couldn't sleep. I cried my eyes out for months thinking you were dead. I'd like to slug you!"

In spite of trying to keep their voices down, the vehemence with which they were carrying on their conversation was starting to draw curious glances from other shoppers.

"I should go," said Lana, willing herself to calm down.

"What about the bank?" he asked.

"I can't do it today," said Lana. "I really did take the locket to be cleaned. I'll pick it up tomorrow morning and meet you at the bank."

"That won't work," said Jeremy. "The compartment was soldered shut. I'd need time to use a torch on it to open it again without damaging the key inside."

"Where do you plan to find one of those?"

"Any reputable hardware store," he told her. "Tell you what, I'll meet you anywhere you would like tomorrow. We'll go back to my motel, and I'll open the locket. Then we'll go to the bank together."

Lana laughed shortly. "You must take me for a fool. If you can work a torch, so can I. I'll open the locket and get the key and we'll meet at the bank tomorrow where there will be security guards with guns on the premises. That way they'll be handy if you try any funny business."

Jeremy placed a hand over his heart. "You cut me with your suspicion, darling. I would never harm a hair on your lovely head."

"Tell it to someone who gives a crap," Lana said, and began pushing her cart toward the front of the store where the cashiers were located.

Jeremy laughed. "You really have changed. But you know, I like the new you. We could have a lot of fun together."

"We've already had all the fun we're ever going to

have. Just tell me the name of the bank and what time you want to meet."

After he gave her all the information she needed, they parted ways.

Chapter 9

When Lana got back to the house, her dad was in the kitchen preparing lunch. He looked up when she entered, and smiled. "Hey, I see you went to the store. Did you remember to get milk?"

"Sure," Lana replied tiredly. The shock of seeing Jeremy so unexpectedly had caught up with her. She felt drained.

"What's the matter?" Aaron asked, putting down the knife he'd been using to slice tomatoes.

Lana met his eyes. "Jeremy accosted me in the supermarket," she told him as tears suddenly flooded her eyes.

Aaron pulled her into his arms. "Where the hell was the FBI?"

"Ten had to go to Norfolk, and his team was supposed to be watching me," she said as she wept. "I was fine until I got in the car and started driving home. Then everything came crashing down. He's really alive, Daddy."

Aaron hugged her tightly. "Oh, sweetie, didn't you know that all along?"

"Yes, I knew it rationally, but to be confronted by the truth was shattering. He used me all those years. I was nothing but a tool, something to help him look trustworthy and respectable."

"I'm sure it was more than that for Jeremy," her father said. "I'm not defending him, but I do believe he loved you in his own way, to the best of his ability. But when it came down to self-preservation or love, love had to lose. Frankly, I'm surprised he ran his con as long as he did. Most con artists move from one con game to the next, never staying too long because that increases the chance of slipping up and getting caught. Maybe he stayed because of you."

Lana wiped her face. "I know you're just trying to make me feel better, but thanks."

Aaron smiled down at her. "No, I really believe that."

The doorbell rang.

"I'll get it," said Lana, sniffling.

Aaron watched as she stood up straighter, and took a deep breath before going to answer the door. She'd been through so much. But she was handling it. His girl was strong.

"Who's there?" Lana called through the door. She'd had one surprise today and wasn't going to let anyone else get the jump on her. She stood in front of the huge oak door with the stained-glass inlay.

"It's Ten," came the familiar voice.

She couldn't get the door open fast enough.

She flew into his arms. "Where were your agents? Jeremy just walked up to me in the produce aisle and I had to wing it!"

She searched his eyes. Ten's were filled with regret.

"Have you been crying?"

"A little," Lana admitted, "but I'm fine. It was weird seeing Jeremy, that's all."

Ten held her tighter. "I'm sorry I wasn't there. The other agents were keeping an eye on who entered and left the store while you were there but they didn't see anyone fitting Corday's description. They thought you were safe. They only learned about your encounter when you told your dad about it a few minutes ago. I told them to get over here, we need to talk."

He released her and Lana shut and locked the door. Then they walked back to the kitchen.

"It's not surprising that your team didn't recognize him. I almost didn't recognize him myself. He's dark-haired now and for some reason that makes all the difference."

"I see," said Ten. But from the tightness of his voice

she knew he really didn't. She sensed he was angry that his team had dropped the ball.

"Seriously, don't be too hard on them. It was an honest mistake," she assured him.

"No, they should have been there for you," Ten asserted. "I leave town for a couple of hours and they fall asleep on the job."

"What did you find out about the locket?" Lana asked, already knowing the answer but wanting to change the subject.

"Oh, yeah," said Ten, reaching into his windbreaker pocket, and retrieving the locket.

"There *was* something inside of it…a safe-deposit-box key."

They walked into the kitchen and Aaron and Ten exchanged hellos, after which Ten and Lana sat down on tall stools at the nearby granite-topped island. Ten gave Lana the locket. "I had the jeweler restore it to its original form after he'd removed the key. I thought it might have sentimental value."

"It used to," Lana said, grasping the once-cherished treasure in her hand and looking down at it a bit sadly. She set it on the countertop.

"Can I see it?"

He handed her the key. Like Jeremy had earlier said, there was nothing distinctive about it. There was a number stamped on the small gold-colored metal key but that was all. She met his eyes. "Do you want to hear about my reunion with my dead husband now or wait until your team gets here?"

"Tell me now," said Ten. "I'll give them the gist of it later on."

Lana handed him back the key and cleared her throat. "I was standing in the produce aisle, looking down at something, I don't remember what now, when I noticed someone had stopped right beside me. Actually, he was standing too close…"

When she was finished relating what had happened, Aaron said, "He's got balls, I'll give him that."

Ten had listened carefully for pertinent information. Jeremy had seemingly given Lana a lot of facts, facts that might lead the Bureau to the missing funds. That was what made him leery. Jeremy had been too generous with the facts. He'd told Lana which bank the safe-deposit box was located in. He'd volunteered that the locket held the key. He'd even suggested a means by which to get the key out of the locket. There had to be a catch.

Suddenly it dawned on him. "Did he say which alias he'd used when he rented the safe-deposit box?"

Lana shook her head in the negative. "No, and I didn't even think to ask him," she said. "Probably because we planned to be together when the box was opened."

"He didn't trust you," Ten told her. "With that information we would have been able to go straight to the box and find out what he's got stashed there. By not telling you the name the box is under he made sure you're going to show up tomorrow."

"What do you think he has in it?" Lana said, curious, "bearer bonds?"

"No," Ten said confidently, "definitely not bearer bonds. The government outlawed the exchange of bearer bonds in the eighties because they were a magnet to any crook who wanted to hide money. They were too easy to transfer from owner to owner, hence their name, bearer bonds.

"I think Jeremy is more than likely dealing in diamonds. Nowadays, they're the going thing with high-level cons like him."

"Diamonds," Lana repeated thoughtfully.

Ten smiled and grasped her hand in his. "Diamonds are a girl's best friend. I must say, you were brilliant making him believe you were on the take."

Lana sighed and said, "He seemed to warm to the wicked side of me."

Ten didn't like the sound of that, but now was not the time to let the green-eyed monster take hold. If they worked this right, Jeremy would be in custody by tomorrow. "You'll wear a wire," he told her. "And all four of us will be nearby."

"Lunch is ready," Aaron announced.

They ate the salads on the back deck where they could look at the ocean while they enjoyed their meal. The field agents arrived while they were in the middle of the meal and Ten and Lana regrettably left Aaron alone on the deck to go speak with them about plans for tomorrow.

This was the first time Lana had met any of them. She greeted them warmly and welcomed them to sit down in the living room. All three agents strode in bearing black cases, which Lana assumed held surveillance equipment and their laptops.

She watched as Pete set up his laptop on the coffee table. He booted it up and quickly typed commands. Turning the screen around so that Lana and Ten could see it, he said, "Here is the footage we shot of the thirty or so minutes you were in the supermarket."

Lana peered closely. The screen showed customers going in and coming out of the busy market. She spotted Jeremy right away because it had been only an hour or so since he'd been standing right in front of her. "That's him," she said, pointing.

Carrie said, "That's the guy I said reminded me of Hugh Jackman. We even joked about it."

Lana squinted at the image that Pete had frozen on the screen. "I suppose he does look a little like Hugh Jackman."

"We apologize for not being more vigilant." Pete spoke for all three of them. Carrie and Eduardo's facial expressions mirrored Pete's sentiments. They were embarrassed by their slipup.

"Like I told Ten," Lana said, letting them off the hook, "I almost didn't recognize him in that disguise myself." Actually she was kind of glad they hadn't heard what she'd said to Jeremy. Some of her comments had been entirely too personal for strangers' ears. She was sure she'd sounded vulnerable and hurt and close to committing a violent act.

"Okay, we've gotten that out of the way," Ten said, eager to get down to business. "Let's talk about how we're going to provide backup for Lana tomorrow."

The technical terms went straight over Lana's head as the agents talked about putting a wire on her, and which of them would be inside the bank posing as customers and who would remain in the van.

More than an hour later Lana was escorting the three field agents to the door. When they were gone, she turned to Ten and smiled up at him. "Does this mean the case is coming to a close?"

"If we're lucky," Ten said, and winked his eye.

She and Ten made it a point of not being too demonstrative with each other in the house, which they knew to be bugged. She wouldn't be surprised to learn the team was not averse to eavesdropping on personal conversations if they were entertaining. Surveillance work was boring, and they probably welcomed anything that broke up the tedium.

Lana risked it anyway by tiptoeing and kissing Ten. "I hope so," she whispered.

Ten bent and deepened the kiss, pressing her close to him.

His mouth devoured Lana's. He heard that sexy sound she made whenever they kissed, a cross be-

tween an exhalation and a moan. His urgency to get
this case over with was mounting in tandem with his
passion for her.

Aaron walked into the living room and saw them
wrapped in each other's arms. He turned around and
went upstairs. He would make himself scarce. Smiling, he decided to phone Ellen and see if she wouldn't
mind an overnight guest. There was a bond develop-
ing between Lana and Ten. He felt a lot better about
Tennison Isles than he'd ever felt about Jeremy Corday or any other guy Lana dated for that matter. He'd
made the mistake of not thoroughly checking Jeremy
out when Lana had first brought him home years ago.
He wouldn't make that mistake twice. Like the thorough, butting in, father he was, he'd had Ten investi-
gated. He was not without friends in high places. One
such friend was a United States senator, and he'd assured him that Ten was everything he'd said he was
and more. The senator had spoken glowingly of Ten's
background, and of his family's dedication to law enforcement both in the military and the private sector.

Ten and Lana were in the living room sitting on the
couch with their heads together talking in whispers
when Aaron came through again on his way out. Lana
looked up at him. He was standing in the doorway with
an overnight bag slung over one shoulder and his laptop in its case over the other. Bowser stood next to him.
"We're spending the night at Ellen's," he announced.

Lana started to say something, but he cut her off

with "That is if you think you'll be safe. I wouldn't want to leave you if you think there's a chance Jeremy will try something tonight."

Now that he'd mentioned it, Lana realized she *couldn't* predict what Jeremy might do. Still, if Jeremy did attempt a second assault on the house she certainly didn't want her father anywhere nearby. "No, I'm covered," she said with a smile. "Have fun, Daddy."

"I plan to," Aaron said. He nodded in Ten's direction. Ten nodded back. That was enough for a silent agreement to be figuratively sealed between the two men. Aaron trusted his only child in his care, and knew Ten wouldn't disappoint him.

Lana jumped up and walked her dad to the door. She held it open for him. "I love you, Daddy."

"Now, don't go saying something like that at a time like this," Aaron said with a smile. "They do that stuff in movies and it never ends well."

She tiptoed and kissed his cheek. "You're way too melodramatic. See you tomorrow, Romeo."

Aaron much preferred her thinking of him as a randy old man, than to be thinking in maudlin terms. "My Juliet's waiting. Come on, boy," he called to Bowser.

He jogged down the steps with Bowser following happily.

Lana shut the door and went back into the living room where she threw herself on top of Ten. "We're alone," she whispered. Enclosing her in his arms and grinning, Ten's head fell back on the couch, and he stretched out. Lana straddled him, the skirt of her sundress riding up her thighs. Their eyes locked. "I don't want to wait any longer," she said breathlessly. "We'll be *very* quiet. I won't scream or shout. I'll be quiet as a mouse."

Ten's penis was already hardening. Her crotch was touching his, and he not only felt the warmth of her, but the little devil was gyrating as if he was inside of her. She licked her lips and threw her head back as if in ecstasy. He could see the imprint of her aroused nipples pressing against the bodice of the sundress. He was not made of stone. How was he supposed to resist something like this?

She bent over him and their lips met in a hungry kiss. Tenderly yet deeply they explored each other, challenging the limits of their control. "You taste so good," Ten murmured against her mouth. Lana softly moaned her pleasure.

Ten reached up and squeezed her butt with both of his big hands. His member was aching to be released from the confines of his jeans. Lana could feel his urgency and reveled in it. Her nipples were erect and becoming painful to the touch. She wanted to be naked. She wanted their bodies hot and slick with perspiration.

She broke off the kiss. Once again sanity reigned. They were in the living room in front of the big picture window. She wasn't about to give Miss Gladys an eyeful. She knew the lovely lady had a telescope, and knew how to use it.

"Bedroom," was her one-word command. She got up and grabbed his hand and led the way. Once through the doorway of her bedroom, clothes began to simply fall off their bodies.

Dressed only in her underwear, Lana went over to the window and pressed a button on the wall. Electric storm windows lowered. No sunlight could penetrate through them, let alone the lens of a certain someone's powerful telescope. She switched on the bedside lamp. Then she went and turned on the CD player. Strains of jazz floated on the air. She turned up the volume just a bit hoping to further hinder them from being heard.

She turned back around to find Ten in his underwear. She had already seen him with his pants off but that was only in swim trunks. The man was well-formed, awesome biceps, pectorals and abdominals. He had a scar about two inches above his waist that looked like it'd been there awhile. Downward, his muscular thighs were beautifully molded and the area where the curly dark hair disappeared into his briefs…she wanted to touch him there.

She went to him, and he reached around and undid her bra. As he freed her breasts from their constraints, they maintained their gravity. When they embraced, she felt such abandon. His warm flesh against hers felt so right.

Biceps flexing, Ten picked her up and carried her

to the bed. They kissed again, this time more urgently than before, and if he wasn't mistaken, he felt tears on her cheeks. This, for a split second, gave him pause. Why was she crying?

But once she was on her back against the bed, and he'd dispensed with her panties and shed his briefs, there was no turning back. He tore open the condom he'd taken out of his pocket downstairs. He was not a newcomer to intimacy and had known this day would be coming soon.

Seconds later the condom was on and he was pushing inside of her. Neither of them spoke. They didn't have to. They clung to each other and rode the tide of passion that had been mounting for days. They got lost in one another's eyes. They both knew this was monumental and not a spur-of-the-moment thing, or something that would soon be forgotten. He started out on top but, after a while, she impaled herself on him. Deep, deep, and so sweetly, she wrapped herself around him.

His hands cupped her luscious breasts. He gently pinched her nipples, heightening her pleasure. Lana rose higher on her knees and began thrusting. With each thrust, Ten grew harder and he marveled at her strength and stamina. Midway, she slowed down, got off him, turned around so that her back was to him. The sight of her backside and consequently her sex almost sent him over the edge. She reached a hand back, took him in it and guided him back inside of her. Then she rode him to climax.

Lana lay on top of him, her feminine center throbbing with release. She moaned softly and he could feel her convulsively tightening and releasing around his shaft. Momentarily, she softly rolled off him and nuzzled in his chest, smiling.

"For a minute there," he whispered as he hugged her close and peered into her upturned face, "I thought you weren't satisfied."

She smiled, her long-lashed eyes sultry. "Wait until I can scream. You'll have no doubts of that whatsoever."

"There wasn't much foreplay," he said, sounding apologetic.

"For me the foreplay begins when you enter the room," she told him.

Ten smiled. "That might be the sweetest thing a woman has ever said to me."

"Sweet, that's me," she whispered against his chest, softly.

Chapter 10

Ten was determined that there would be no screwups today. It was a beautiful day for a capture. The Carolina sky was baby blue with a smattering of clouds but none appeared rain producing. When he and Pete pulled across the street in the van that morning, pedestrians were already out and about. The bank sat on the corner, taking up much of the downtown block. It was a four-story modern edifice with a marble facade and had a Southern touch with pillars on either side of the entrance.

Carrie and Eduardo had been chosen to pose as customers. Ten couldn't do it because Jeremy would recognize him as Lana's "boyfriend," and the sting would be over with before it'd begun.

Ten had fitted Lana with the wire, and had advised her to "Try to forget you have it on. It's best that way. Otherwise you might inadvertently touch that spot too frequently or behave conspicuously. Jeremy's already paranoid. We don't want him to suspect you've betrayed him."

"I know," she said, looking into his eyes. "I should stick to the script."

"Which is?" he prompted.

"Go in, give him the key. He'll probably have to go into the vault with a bank employee who will also have a key. They will both have to open the box together.

"After that, Jeremy gets whatever's in the box and comes out of the vault. I'll be waiting for him. Then he will either give me my share of the loot or he'll try to run with all of it. Either way, you all will pounce on him and give him the beat-down he so richly deserves."

He chuckled at her use of the phrase *beat-down*. "You sound like a gangster's moll," he joked. "And we'll try our best to avoid violence."

She looked at him with such affection that a lump formed in his throat.

A few moments later, he and Pete watched as she walked into the bank dressed to kill wearing a short dark brown dress, which was hitting on all her curves, and brown pumps. She wore designer sunglasses and carried a brown handbag that matched the shoes. Her red hair set the whole outfit off. He smiled, shaking his head. She had style.

"Man," Pete said in admiration. "She's wearing the *hell* outta that dress."

"Keep your mind on the job," Ten said gruffly.

Pete threw up his hands. "I'm just saying…"

Next, Carrie went into the bank followed by Eduardo a couple minutes later. Last, Ten spotted Jeremy casually stroll into the bank, wearing dress slacks and a short-sleeved dress shirt with a tie. His black oxfords were highly polished.

Inside, Lana walked up to Jeremy as soon as he entered the lobby. His blue eyes swept over her. "Good morning, sweetness," he said, smiling confidently. "You look quite fetching in your power attire."

Lana handed him the key. "Let's get this over with," she said without rancor. She didn't want to appear antagonistic. She simply wasn't going to engage in friendly banter with him.

"All right," he said easily as he palmed the key. "I'll only be a few minutes."

Lana walked over to a counter that was stocked with deposit slips, withdrawal slips and various brochures touting the bank's services. She picked up a brochure, but she didn't allow her attention to wander from Jeremy as he walked up to an employee's desk.

The middle-aged man rose and offered his hand for Jeremy to shake and gestured to the chair in front of his desk. Jeremy bestowed a charming smile on the man and sat down, after which he produced the key and began to tell the man why he was there.

Lana couldn't hear what they were saying but Jeremy's pantomime was sufficient for her to follow what was going on. After Jeremy had shown the employee adequate identification the man rose and left the lobby. When he returned he said something to Jeremy. Jeremy rose and walked with the employee toward the back of the bank. They disappeared through a door. Lana took the opportunity to station herself at that very door to await Jeremy's return.

In the vault Jeremy and the bank employee used their keys to unlock the safe-deposit box. The bank employee said, "I'll give you some privacy," and left the vault.

Jeremy carried the box to a nearby table, and lifted the lid. He took a deep breath. He'd been waiting so long for this moment. Unable to wait another second he reached in and grasped a black-velvet drawstring bag. His heart hammered in his chest as he untied the knot in the string, opened the bag and poured a handful of clear-as-crystal diamonds, all of them well over ten carats, into his hand. The excitement he felt was better than sex. Better than that first inkling that you were falling in love with that special someone. This was the high he lived for, that he would die for if it ever came down to it.

He reluctantly poured the diamonds back into the bag. Lana was waiting. Maybe he would still try to convince her to go away with him. He could forgive her dalliance with the mystery man caught by his private detective. He hadn't exactly been a saint during their separation. As for love, well, he loved her as much as he could ever love any woman. He certainly loved her more than he'd loved his first two wives. He'd stayed longer with her than the both of them put together. Giving her all of him, though, was out of the question. They could have fun together. Splurge on life. Go anywhere they wanted to. Live in the lap of luxury.

He tucked the drawstring bag into the briefcase and left the vault. Once in the corridor, he looked for the bank employee but he wasn't anywhere in sight so he started back the way he'd come. He saw Lana as soon as he was through the door.

He smiled and patted the briefcase.

She didn't crack a smile. "Let's find a private corner and divvy up the prize," she said instead.

But Jeremy had another idea. "No, babe, let's go straight to Norfolk. The buyer is meeting me at the Radisson tomorrow morning. We could spend the night and catch up while we wait on him."

Lana's mind was racing. He already had a buyer. But of course he did. He'd planned this down to the minutest detail. Her eyes darted around her, and as soon as she did that she regretted it because Jeremy, attuned to everything in his heightened state of excitement, noticed the gesture and immediately became suspicious. "Who're you looking for, your new boy-

friend? Did you two plan to rob me?" He searched the
bank's lobby for Ten.

"Jeremy, don't be silly, you're paranoid," Lana said
calmly, her voice barely a whisper. She sighed as if she
were growing annoyed with him. "Look, we made a
deal. It didn't involve going anywhere else with you.
You said nothing about a buyer yesterday. We were
supposed to split whatever was in the safe-deposit box,
and go our separate ways, remember?"

Jeremy's eyes lost their frightened aspect. He was
clutching the briefcase handle tightly in his right hand.
He relaxed. "You're right, we did agree to split whatever's in here, but that's not reasonable, Lana. What
do you know about finding a buyer for millions of dollars' worth of diamonds? I've got this under control.
Go with me on this, and you'll be set for life."

Lana saw no logical reason to argue the point with
him. Carrie was only five feet away from them, pretending to fill out a form. Eduardo was sitting in a
chair near the exit, apparently waiting to be called to
the desk of a loan officer.

She should simply play along with Jeremy until they
got outside, at which point Ten and Pete would wrestle
him to the ground and it would all be over with.

"Okay," she said at last. "I'll go to Norfolk with
you." She opened her purse and withdrew a small black
canister. "But if you try anything I'm going to pep-
per spray you."

Jeremy laughed shortly. "Deal," he said. He took

her arm and guided her toward the exit. But before he could place his hand on the glass door, Eduardo shouted, "FBI! You're under arrest!"

Lana fell back, putting some distance between her and Jeremy. Jeremy swung the briefcase over and up, hitting Eduardo under the chin. Blood spouted from Eduardo's mouth. Carrie lunged for Jeremy's midsection, throwing her whole body into it. Jeremy went down with her on top of him. However, Jeremy was stronger than she was and tossed her off of him and rose quickly. On his feet now, he executed a roundhouse kick, and sent her sprawling against one of the counters. She hit her head and was knocked out. Everything happened in an instant.

In the meantime, Eduardo was on the floor, bleeding, dazed, as his eyes tried to focus. Jeremy had not only knocked some teeth loose with that briefcase to the chin move, but had also made him bite his tongue, which was producing copious amounts of blood.

Lana, horrified, tried to run to Carrie to see if she was all right because she hadn't stirred once since she'd hit her head on the counter, but Jeremy angrily wrenched her back, pulled her to his side and dragged her toward the exit.

"You must be insane, attacking FBI agents!" she cried, trying to pull free of his hold. But his grip was too firm. She hoped Ten and Pete were on the ball and listening to his every word. No, she hoped they were already out of the van and waiting outside for Jeremy with guns drawn.

"So sorry, darling, but I don't plan on going to jail. Didn't faking my death teach you anything?" Jeremy said through clenched teeth.

Around them bank customers and employees were cowering behind counters, trying to make themselves as invisible to the madman as possible. Lana wondered where the security guards were. In answer to her question, two security guards hurried toward them from the back. One looked like he had to be in his sixties or seventies. His hair was cottony-white and his tanned face held deep wrinkles, but he moved sprightly enough. As he approached them he held up his hands to show he only wanted to talk. "Young fellow," he said soothingly. "Let's maintain a cool head here, and talk about what we can do to get you to let the lady go and be on your way out of here, free and clear. No harm, no foul, okay?" He nodded encouragingly as he smiled at Jeremy.

The younger security guard hung back but his hand was on his weapon in its holster at his side. His thumb was already on the release snap that would free his weapon should he need to draw.

Jeremy held Lana tightly against his chest with the same hand in which he held the briefcase. The hard handle was digging painfully into her chest. Even drawing a deep breath was difficult. His breath, coming in quick intervals, was in her ear. "No," he told the white-haired security guard. "The lady comes with me."

"My name's Hiram," the security guard said conversationally. He walked a little closer and as he did so, keeping his eyes on Jeremy's eyes, he released the thumb break snap on his holster. "I've been working here nearly twenty years and we've never had any trouble. I don't want any trouble today. Just let go of the lady, and I'll let you walk right out of here. I promise you."

Jeremy smiled. "I wasn't born yesterday, Hiram. The lady's my ticket out of here."

Hiram inched a little closer. "I know you think that, son. But so far all you've done is hit a couple of people, if you leave this bank with her that'll be kidnapping."

"She's my wife," said Jeremy. "A man can't kidnap his own wife."

"We're divorced," Lana said her voice strangled.

"Is that what this is?" asked Hiram, "a domestic dispute?" He smiled as if he were relieved that's all this was about. "You know women, son. They don't respond to rough handling. Let her go."

Jeremy tensed. Lana, who was pressed against him, felt his muscles flex in the direction they eventually moved before he actually did what he was getting ready to do. But she had no way of preventing his actions. He'd snatched the gun out of Hiram's holster and shoved him to the floor before Hiram had time to react.

The younger security guard pulled his gun. "Drop it, mister!"

Jeremy laughed. "I think not," he said as he backed toward the exit with Lana. "Let's try this again, shall we?"

"I'm warning you," cried the younger security guard, "I'll shoot if you don't drop your weapon."

"No you won't," said Jeremy confidently. "You're only some police-academy dropout who's so scared you're about to pee yourself. The old guy had more nerve."

He was right. The younger security guard was trembling so hard he had difficulty maintaining the stance required to shoot accurately. Lana was praying he wouldn't shoot just to prove Jeremy wrong because she feared she would be the one getting hit. "Jeremy, please, let me go. I'm just slowing you down."

"Be quiet, I need to think," Jeremy hissed.

They were through the door. Looking back into the bank, Lana saw Carrie being helped off the floor by Eduardo who was talking into his cell phone. Lana assumed he was in contact with Ten or Pete.

Jeremy jerked her around so that she was in front of him. "Oh, for God's sake!" he exclaimed when he saw Ten standing about six feet away, his gun trained on him. "He's FBI, too?" he asked Lana.

Lana was mute. She had just gotten a good look at the gun in Jeremy's hand. It was a .38, nothing fancy, but a good solid weapon. She'd used one on a gun range plenty of times. Her dad had given her one for her twenty-first birthday soon after she announced she was moving to California to pursue a career in interior design. "It's the perfect accessory," he'd joked. "It goes with anything."

She wanted to smile, but kept her facial expression neutral. Jeremy obviously didn't know very much about handguns. The one he was holding still had the safety on. Good old Hiram was a stickler for safety, bless his heart.

"Drop the weapon, Corday," Ten ordered.

Jeremy ignored him. "You're dating an FBI man… on purpose?" Jeremy said in Lana's ear.

"What's it to you?" she said, trying to provoke him. If she got him angry enough maybe his mind wouldn't let him add up the blatant coincidences that had led him to this moment.

Lana glanced directly at Ten, but his attention was trained on Jeremy. She willed Ten to look at her. He shifted his gaze to her and she quickly glanced at the gun in Jeremy's hand and wrinkled her brow as if to say, "Take a good look at the weapon." Unfortunately she wasn't as good with telepathy as she thought so Ten wasn't picking up on her signals.

"I mean, that kiss couldn't have been a fake, could it?" Jeremy asked. He was talking to himself now.

"Jeremy, stay on track," Lana said. "Diamonds, escape, Tahiti, or wherever you're going to spend the rest of your life on the run."

"You set me up!" he screamed. Enlightenment dawned on him at the most inopportune moment that Lana could imagine.

Ten steeled himself, his stance firm, his aim true. If Corday so much as twitched, he was a dead man.

Pete was to the left of him ready to back him up.

Carrie and Eduardo were behind Corday, off to the side out of the line of fire, their weapons also at the ready. They were visibly battered, and in Eduardo's case, bloody, but both were steady on their feet and clearheaded.

"I can't believe you conned me," Jeremy said incredulously. No one interrupted him. He continued in a more reasonable tone. "In a way, I'm glad he's only your fake boyfriend. And you didn't sleep with him." He paused. He squeezed her tighter and peered into her face. "You didn't sleep with him, did you?"

Lana thought it best not to answer. He was beginning to scare her. Would he really shoot her if she refused to cooperate with him? She had to make a move soon or he might get wise to the fact that the safety was still on the .38.

"Lana, did you sleep with him?" he demanded.

"Corday, she's terrified," Ten said. "Put the weapon down and let her go."

Jeremy had not been pointing the .38 at anyone but now he aimed at Ten. "I should put a bullet in your head," he threatened.

With his focus on Ten, Jeremy relaxed his hold on

Lana for a moment and she stomped hard on his foot with her heel and simultaneously turned and hit him in the nose with her fist. Free now, she ran behind Ten, yelling, "The safety's still on!"

Jeremy, figuring he had nothing left to lose, took aim and tried to fire at Ten. Nothing happened. Then what Lana had said must have registered because he attempted to click off the safety. However, in the next split second, Ten was on him, delivering a punch to the side of his head.

Jeremy's legs went weak under him. He dropped everything he'd been holding on to, both the gun and the briefcase. He wobbled and fell to his knees, then onto his side, hitting the back of his head on the pavement.

Stepping forward, Ten shoved the gun out of the prone man's reach with his foot. He squatted next to Jeremy and turned his face around so that he could get a good look at him. He was out cold. "Pete," he said, "Cuff him, and then call the paramedics."

Eduardo and Carrie rushed out of the bank. Eduardo bent and picked up the gun. Carrie went to Lana. "Are you all right?" she asked concerned.

Lana hugged her whether she wanted to be hugged or not, to hell with FBI protocol. She'd earlier thought Jeremy had fatally injured the poor woman and was relieved to see her on her feet again.

"Am *I* all right?" Lana cried. "The question is, are *you* all right?"

"I'm a tough bird," Carrie said, smiling.

Sirens sounded in the distance. Lana scanned the scene. Pete was cuffing Jeremy, who looked to be regaining consciousness. Eduardo was talking to the two security guards, and Ten had picked up the briefcase, and was walking toward her.

"Excuse me," said Carrie as Ten approached. She hurried over to help Pete get Jeremy off the ground.

Ten smiled at Lana. "You continue to amaze me. Not many people would've recognized the safety was still on. But amazement aside, that was a risky move. It scared me. If anything had happened to you…" He trailed off not wanting to voice what horrors the scenario presented for him.

Lana was incredibly relieved it was finally over. Jeremy was in custody. Ten was safe. No one had gotten irreparably injured. She had to restrain herself from throwing herself into Ten's arms. He was working. She wouldn't think of embarrassing him.

"Here we are at the close of the case," she said in low tones. "You've got your man and what I'm guessing is over two hundred million in diamonds. I would call that a job well done, Special Agent Isles. Notice I'm not being too familiar with you."

"Screw that," said Ten. He pulled her into his arms and kissed her soundly.

When he let her go, Lana was starry-eyed.

Jeremy had seen them as Pete walked him over to the paramedic's van. He angrily tossed off, "You cheating whore!"

Lana laughed. "We're divorced!" she reminded him gleefully.

Ten took her by the hand and escorted her to the surveillance van. Inside, he opened the briefcase and took out the pouch filled with diamonds. "I thought you'd like to see what you just risked your life for," he said as he poured the diamonds into her cupped hands.

"Wow," Lana breathed, admiring all the sparkly stones. "I can see why people go nuts over these things." She hastily poured them back into the bag. "Get them away from me. I can feel wicked Lana trying to break through. She wants a new Ferrari and a vacation house on the Riviera," she joked.

Ten laughed, and drew the drawstring shut, then put the diamonds back in the briefcase. "The money from the sale of these babies is going to make a lot of retirees happy."

Chapter 11

"I can't believe Jeremy didn't have a clue about the safety," Aaron said later that evening as they all sat on the deck at his house. After Lana returned from the bank she'd phoned her dad and told him she was safe and Jeremy was in custody. That's when Aaron suggested a party to celebrate the event. "Invite the whole gang, if they can make it," he'd said.

Lana had made no promises, then, because quite a few details had to be worked out following the arrest. The local police showed up because a panicked bank employee phoned them. Ten was obliged to explain the actions of the FBI in the local police's jurisdiction. They were not pleased they weren't informed about the sting beforehand. Especially since they were going to house Jeremy in their jail until Ten made travel arrangements with the U.S. Marshals for him to go back to San Francisco to face his accusers. Plus, Carrie, Eduardo and herself had to be examined by paramedics. Lana had protested but was told she might be suffering from shock. These things had a way of sneaking up on you when you least expected it. She gave in and let them check her blood pressure and heart rate. She was more worried about Carrie and Eduardo, who were advised to go to the hospital for tests due to receiving head injuries.

Finally, because Jeremy had used her as a human shield she was required to give a statement to the police on the scene, after which Ten pulled her aside, "You should go home now, Lana. I'm going to be a while. First with getting Jeremy situated, then going to the hospital to make sure Jenkins and Como are all right."

Lana *was* tired. She was experiencing a strange lethargy, maybe from the result of the waning adrenaline rush. "Only if you promise to call me after you find out how Carrie and Eduardo are."

"You've got it," Ten agreed, and kissed her cheek. "Go get some rest. You were a rock today."

Lana hadn't felt strong and competent today. At times she was terrified with Jeremy breathing down her neck and yelling in her ear like a madman. She gave Ten a wan smile and left.

Outside the street was mercifully clear of news

vans. Thank God for small towns. If this were San Francisco she wouldn't have been able to get to her car.

Ten sat in the back of the police cruiser with Jeremy as they were driven to the local police station by an officer. Jeremy was cuffed as he stared straight ahead, his expression unreadable. He turned his head to regard Ten. "Isn't there some rule against an agent getting involved with a suspect's wife? Because if there isn't, there should be. What did you have to do to get her to cooperate?"

Ten considered not engaging in conversation with Jeremy. He certainly didn't owe him an explanation. However he wanted to make it abundantly clear to him that he was responsible for this situation, and no one else.

"You're caught, Davis. Yes, we know your real name. It's time you stopped deluding yourself. You committed a criminal act and now you're going to pay for it. How did I get Lana to cooperate? It's simple. You pissed her off. I had to rein her in, she was so eager to get even with you. So you have no one to blame but yourself."

Jeremy smiled coolly. "Do you think she'll settle for a Boy Scout like you after she's had me? No, she'll forgive me and wait for me while I serve my time."

"Whatever gets you through the night," Ten said. It was apparent to him that Jeremy Davis was not ready to give up his delusions.

For the remainder of the trip to the police station he explained to Davis that the U.S. Marshals would be escorting him back to San Francisco where he would stand trial.

"You don't have to hold our hands," Carrie told Ten later as they sat in the examination room at the hospital. The doctor had agreed to see Carrie and Eduardo together after he'd been told they were FBI, and had been hurt in the line of duty. There were certain perks that came with the badge.

Eduardo, whose tongue was swollen, wasn't saying much of anything. When he did the words were incoherent. Pete stood nearby, too. They often said disparaging things to one another while on duty but when a man was down they stuck together.

The doctor had already seen to Eduardo, and was now stitching closed the cut over Carrie's right eye. "Hopefully you won't have a scar," he said. "But if you do it'll be one of those cool eyebrow scars."

Carrie smiled at him.

"I suppose when you're in my line of work scars are inevitable," she said.

The doctor smiled, "Your husband must worry about you all the time."

"I'm not married, are you?"

"No," he said, and blushed.

"Look," Eduardo mumbled, "if you two want to be alone, we'll wait outside."

"I didn't understand a word you said," Carrie told him. Then she returned her attention to the dreamy doctor.

Ten could only smile at their exchange. Eduardo had been trying to get Carrie to go out with him for months. Ever since Carrie's divorce had become final. But Carrie wouldn't give him the time of day. He knew that Eduardo had been interested in her before the divorce but out of respect for her marriage had not said anything. Now, he had to watch her flirt with another man? It was probably eating him up.

Fraternizing in the Bureau was frowned upon. However many were not sticklers about the rules. Ten knew of several relationships among agents, even some marriages.

"Excuse me," Ten said to his colleagues, "I promised to phone Lana after I found out if you two were going to live."

Since the hospital had a rule against the use of cell phones in certain areas, he'd followed the corridors to the first floor lobby, where they were permitted. He'd pulled up her number on his phone. With a press of a button, her phone started ringing.

At her dad's house, Lana was in the kitchen shucking sweet corn. Her dad and Ellen were adamant about throwing the party whether there were two guests or ten. Aaron had already phoned the local fish market, and had them deliver ten pounds of shrimp for the shrimp boil. He was out on the back deck now firing up the gas boiler. Lana and Ellen were relegated to getting the shrimp ready for the pot, preparing the corn and washing the red potatoes that would go in the pot, too.

She dried her hands, checked the display and quickly answered, "Hi. How is everything?"

"Looking up," Ten said. "Jenkins and Como have minor injuries. They should be able to fly tomorrow."

On her end, Lana's heart skipped a beat. Tomorrow, he'd said. "Oh, you have to leave that soon?"

"I'm afraid so. Arrangements have been made. We have an 11:00-a.m. flight out of Norfolk."

"Well, what are you doing tonight?" Lana asked. "Because Dad just invited all of you here for a shrimp boil."

"I'm game," Ten said without hesitation. "I'll ask the others and let you know."

"Okay, bye!"

Ten went back to the examination room with a smile on his face. He met his team as they were leaving the room. "How would you like to go to a party at Aaron Braithwaite's house?" he said.

"If it involves food, I'm there," said Carrie, "although Eduardo may not be able to eat much. I'll eat his share."

Eduardo mumbled something.

"He'd love to," Carrie answered for him, laughing.

Pete laughed. "Me, too," he said. "I love his books and was hoping I'd get the chance to meet him."

It was settled. Ten phoned Lana back and told her everyone was coming.

Music and laughter wafted on the air as dusk fell. With the sun setting, the breezes off the Atlantic became cooler and Lana enjoyed the feel of them on her skin. She and Ten stood talking quietly on the far corner of the deck separated from the others. She was wearing a white cotton dirndl skirt and a sleeveless black blouse. She'd taken off her sandals.

Ten had on jeans and a white short-sleeved shirt. She'd convinced him to take a walk on the beach with her earlier so he was barefoot, too.

"So, what happens now?" she asked softly, her eyes on his.

He could see by the sultry look she gave him that she was referring to the two of them, not the next step in Jeremy's case. Ten didn't know what to tell her. He knew how he felt. He wanted her in his life. However, he also knew she'd been through an emotional upheaval. He should be man enough to give her some space, time to figure out what she wanted.

"That's entirely up to you," he told her in a tone equally softly.

She tilted her head, looking slightly confused by his response. "Aren't you in this, too?"

"Yes, and no," Ten said.

"What do you mean, yes and no?" she asked.

"I only meant that I'll understand if you need some time alone," Ten said gently.

Lana turned away in a huff. "You're confusing me even more. You could have said when we get back to San Francisco you'll call and we'll actually go on a date. I'm not asking for the moon. I just want to know that what we have is not something spur of the moment, or solely physical."

Ten sighed, and grabbed her by the arm, turning her around to face him again. "I think you already know that's not what this is. I want you. Hell, I can see you in my life forever, but what I want doesn't count. Emotions are running high right now. You've probably not even had time to sort out your feelings about Jeremy. You just got divorced. You need time for you, Lana. I'll be there when, or if, you're ready for me."

"Is that it? Seeing me with Jeremy gave you cold feet about you and me?" Lana asked. "I'm over Jeremy. I've had months to come to the realization that he used me for years. What we had was based on lies. I want the truth in my life now."

Ten smiled sadly. "Something simpler, you mean? Well, with me that's what you would get. I'm definitely not rich, or a charmer, and on my salary there would be no extravagant jewels or mansions. I can't offer you any of that."

Lana was beginning to see red. "If you think I was with Jeremy for what he could give me, you're dead wrong! I guess your researchers did a poor job on my

background before I met him. I was already a successful, sought-after designer. I married him because I fell
in love with him. Yeah, that's something I've come to
regret, but that intitial love was genuine. You don't
have to bring up the fact that my judgment is question-
able because of it. I've already pretty much tortured
myself over that. But I'm not somehow emotionally
damaged as a result, either."

"I never said you were emotionally damaged," Ten
disavowed. "Just that you should take time to explore
your feelings."

About fifty feet away on the other end of the deck,
Ellen, who had glanced up and seen Lana and Ten's
body language, asked Aaron, "Are they arguing?"

Aaron, about to twist the cap off a bottle of beer,
looked skeptical. "More like making plans for the rest
of their lives. Those two are in love, mark my words."

Ellen frowned. "Lana looks like she's about to hit
him to me."

Aaron took a careful look in their direction. Lana
was very expressive with her hands, sure, but she didn't
appear to be belligerent. He couldn't hear what they
were saying because they were keeping their voices
down.

Suddenly, Lana walked off, hands on hips, her stride
determined. Okay, well, now he knew she was angry.
That was her pissed-off walk. "I think you're right,"
he said to Ellen. "Something's wrong in paradise."

Lana, who'd earlier noticed Eduardo was not capable of chewing the shrimp and the corn on the cob without experiencing pain, had fixed him some soft scrambled eggs and toast to eat. That had been easier for him to handle. Now, as she approached their table she smiled at Eduardo, and said, "Do you eat ice cream? You're not lactose intolerant are you?"

Eduardo smiled. "Sure," he said. It sounded like something else entirely but Lana got his meaning.

"How about a vanilla milkshake?" she asked. "I feel so bad you haven't been able to eat much because of your injury."

Eduardo rose. "I'll help," he said. He took a furtive glance at Carrie before leaving the table, hoping his going inside alone with Lana would make her jealous.

Carrie burped softly. She had indeed done her part to eat his share of the shrimp. Dessert sounded good to her. "Could you make me a dish of vanilla ice cream? Don't bother with the shake."

Lana smiled. "Of course," she said, "Anyone else want a dish of ice cream or a shake?"

No one else did.

In the kitchen as Lana went to the freezer to get the ice cream, she said to Eduardo, "How long have you and Carrie worked together?"

He held up three fingers.

"Three years, huh?" she said sympathetically.

He nodded in the affirmative.

"How long have you been in love with her?"

He held up three fingers.

Lana laughed briefly. "She's a tough nut to crack?"

Eduardo pretended to twist a ring on his ring finger. Then he pretended to take off the ring and fling it across his shoulder.

"You recently got divorced?" Lana asked.

He shook his head, then with a nod of his head gestured to Carrie out on the deck.

"Oh, *she* got divorced."

He nodded in the affirmative.

Lana put three scoops of ice cream into the blender and added enough milk to cover the ice cream, which was a homemade recipe. It was made with honey instead of sugar and grated vanilla, so the vanilla taste was fresh and delicious.

In moments it was blended and then she poured it into a tall glass and put a straw in it for Eduardo. She watched as he tasted it. "Mmm," he said, smiling.

"I'm glad you like it," said Lana, feeling calmer now. Her mother used to say that a sure way to improve your mood was to do something nice for someone else.

She dished up a bowl of ice cream for Carrie, put the ice cream back in the freezer, then she and Eduardo joined the others once more.

When they got to the table, Carrie took one look at Eduardo's milkshake and said, "Man, that looks good, may I?" And she took it right out of his hand and sipped it.

Lana knew then that Carrie obviously liked Eduardo a lot. She just enjoyed making him suffer with her show of disinterest.

"That's like heaven in a glass," Carrie said. She smiled at Eduardo. "That ought to be soothing on your tongue, big guy."

Eduardo smiled back. Seeing that made Lana's throat grow tight with emotion. Love was beautiful to watch.

Ten was still on the opposite end of the deck, alone. She walked over to rejoin him. The sun was now disappearing on the horizon. They stood gazing at it, not saying anything for a while. Then she broke the silence.

"All right. I'm going to stay here awhile. You can call me if you like."

"I'd like," he said.

"In the meanwhile, I'll be searching my soul," she said, trying to keep the sarcasm out of her tone even though that's how she felt about the notion that she didn't know her own heart. But if it made him certain she wanted him, government salary and all, then she was willing to make the sacrifice.

After all, when it came to real time, they had known each other only a week or so. Even if it felt like a lot longer. Which was his point, emotions were certainly running high.

Bowser appeared at her side, tail wagging hopefully. "He wants a walk," Lana explained to Ten. "Want to join us?"

* * *

As they walked along the beach Bowser ran into the surf, making a game of avoiding the water as the waves chased him back ashore.

Lana laughed at him. "He's such a nut."

"You adore him."

"I do," Lana agreed. Lana placed her hand in his as they strolled. "I love everything about this place. I feel complete here."

"Because you're loved here," Ten said.

She smiled up at him. "It feels as if it's more than just love. When I'm here I feel in sync with the ocean and the air and the land. As if it's in my genes. I can't fully explain the feeling."

"It's where you belong."

"Yes, that's close to it. But it's also as if here is where I feel strongest. When I come home I'm recharged, fortified. Then I go back to San Francisco with a fresh perspective and with resolve to be happy. To be the best I can be."

"I never really thought about it, but I get what you're saying," Ten said. "I always feel uplifted when I go home to see my family. I haven't seen them in a while."

"Everything you told me about your family was true?" Lana asked. "You really are the tenth child?"

"All true," Ten said. "The men in my family are very virile and the women very fertile. It's a win-win situation."

Lana laughed. "You said every one of your brothers and sisters have children except you."

"That's right. I never found the right woman," Ten said. "I do want children. I want the traditional arrangement, marriage first, a child later, and two parents who love each other raising the kid."

"We agree there," Lana told him.

"A child would be a big comfort to you now," Ten guessed.

Lana felt herself on the verge of tears after he said that. Maybe he was right and she had emotions that needed to be addressed. "I try not to think about what might have been," she said. "It doesn't change the facts. But, yes, I do love children and I'd like to have some one day."

"How many?" asked Ten.

"At least two," Lana said. "I wouldn't want my child to grow up lonely like I did. I would've given my right arm for a brother or sister when I was growing up. Daddy says I had an imaginary friend when I was really young, around three or four. Funny, I don't remember that. Maybe we block certain things," she giggled. "How many do you want?"

"Four or five," said Ten with conviction.

"Why not go for ten?" she joked.

"Because I doubt any woman in her right mind today would be willing to have that many," he said with conviction. His eyes held an amused expression.

He suddenly stopped walking, and pulled her into

his arms. He took her face between his large hands and for several seconds just looked deeply into her eyes. "You're so beautiful." And then, he kissed her.

After they parted Lana smiled up at him. "I'd be willing to meet you halfway and go for five."

Ten laughed softly. "Be careful what you say. I have a very good memory."

"Well, remember this while you're in San Francisco and I'm here," she said, getting up on her tiptoes to plant a very sensual kiss on his lips. It was slow and deep and rocked him to his core. He wondered how in the world he was going to get on that plane tomorrow and leave her behind. Let alone spend however many weeks apart until she returned to San Francisco.

Chapter 12

Ten reported to Special Agent In Charge Kagen at the field office on Golden Gate Avenue. He thought he was going to get a reprimand for the manner in which he'd handled the case, however before he could even sit down Kagen instead exclaimed, "Good job, Ten. Your methods were a bit unorthodox but you got Corday, and located the missing funds. That was our objective, so we're going to ignore that you broke a couple rules in the process. In fact, I'm recommending you as my replacement. I'm going to the Sacramento office. Word hasn't come down from the top yet as to who'll be the next special-agent-in-charge, but with your record you stand a good chance."

"Thank you, sir," said Ten, more than a little surprised.

Kagen then gestured to the chair in front of his desk. "Sit, there's something I'd like to talk with you about and this is not Bureau business, it's personal."

Ten took a seat, wondering where this was leading. But he didn't have to wonder too long.

"I realize that your behavior on this case stemmed from your personal feelings for Corday's wife, um, ex-wife, I was recently informed. It's not the first time an agent has developed feelings for a subject. We have them under surveillance for months, which gives us a bird's-eye view of their lives. You're human. You begin to sympathize with them. And these feelings can feel genuine. But after the case is over, you come to your senses and conclude that it was infatuation. Like a summer fling, brief but intense. Do you understand me?"

Of course Ten understood him. He was saying the case was over and done with, and it was time to stop behaving like a lovesick schoolboy, leave Lana Corday alone and get on with Bureau business.

Ten said, "I do understand you. But, I'd like something clarified. Is it against Bureau protocol if I date Lana Corday?"

"No—the case is officially over," said Kagen.

"That's good," said Ten, "because what I have with Lana isn't any of those things you described. I'm serious about her."

Kagen smiled slowly. "I know how hard it is for us to maintain a good relationship, Ten. So, actually, I'm glad to hear that, and I'm happy for you. Good luck."

He rose and offered Ten his hand. Pleased with the way the conversation had gone, Ten gratefully shook it. "Thank you."

Lana tried her best to immerse herself in Outer Banks life and forget about the desire, lurking just below the surface, to hop on the next plane to San Francisco. She socialized with the girls—Bobbi Lee, Siobhan, Gayle and Anastasia. She took long walks on the beach with Bowser and her dad, and kept running. But she no longer had the compulsion to run her troubles away.

Ten kept his promise and phoned her every night. He told her that Jeremy had been denied bail. The judge said he'd proven he was a flight risk, so they weren't even going to give him the opportunity to try it again.

One night, about three weeks after Ten and his team had captured Jeremy, Lana asked Ten if he thought she would be called as a witness at Jeremy's trial. "I doubt it," he'd told her. "What happened after he skipped bail won't have any bearing on his trial. He's going to have to answer for the former charges. Of course, if you want to press charges against him for what he did to you, that's your prerogative."

"The bank isn't pressing charges?"

"The bank is leaving it up to the FBI to see that he's punished. No one was hurt and they're letting it go," Ten explained.

"How generous of them," Lana said, sounding disappointed. "I understand their reasoning though. If he's prosecuted to the full extent of the law, he should go to jail for a long time. So I guess I'll follow their example, save myself the headaches, and not press charges, either."

"I'm sure he'll appreciate it," said Ten with a note of sarcasm.

Lana chuckled. "Yeah, he'll probably send me a handwritten thank-you note."

Changing the subject, Ten asked, "How goes the soul-searching?"

"My soul's been turned every which way but loose," Lana joked. "I'm pretty sure I'm as spiritually centered as the Dalai Lama by now."

Ten laughed. "Good, because I miss you something awful."

"Sometimes I can hear that little boy from Virginia in your voice," she said huskily.

"I'm afraid that country boy will always be a part of me." Ten didn't try to deny it. "He's honest and true, and he's in love with you."

"And he's somewhat of a poet," Lana said, her smile widening even more. He'd said he loved her. She was slightly embarrassed by how happy that made her.

"This country girl loves you, too," she told him. "A whole heap."

His soft laughter made her heart do a flip-flop. "Just tell me when you're coming home, and I'll pick you up at the airport," he promised.

She wasted no time telling him. She'd booked her flight that morning, knowing she was going back to San Francisco whether he thought she was ready for him or not. *She* knew. She'd known three weeks ago. Being at her father's house had afforded her time to reinforce her certainty. She couldn't forever be second-guessing herself when it came to her choice in men. Jeremy had been a bad choice. However, none of the other men in her life, the ones who counted, like her dad, had ever disappointed her. Even her dad's decision to cooperate with the FBI in order to lure her back home hadn't made her lose faith in him. She'd known he'd done it with her best interests at heart. So, now, she would have faith in her relationship with Ten.

She arrived in town on a Saturday afternoon. Ten was there in the waiting area of her carrier when she landed. Their eyes met across the room, and she ran to him. He picked her up and squeezed her tightly in his strong arms. The pure joy at seeing him again suffused her body, and she sighed with pleasure.

She slid down the length of his body. Looking into his eyes, she simply appreciated the wonder that was her Ten. That's when he lowered his head and kissed her. Kissed her like her lips were sustenance and he was damned near starvation. She tingled all over. When they came up for air, she gave a little contented sigh, and they left the terminal hand in hand.

On the drive to her apartment, she told him her father and Ellen sent their best. He smiled at her. "I think your father's made his choice."

"He hasn't said anything about being in love, but I think so, too," she agreed. "They're inseparable. She's retired from teaching, and if she isn't at his place, he's at hers. I've never known him to be this into anyone else since my mom."

"How do you feel about that? Not upset that you'll have to share him?"

Lana laughed. "Of course not," she said, "I just want him to be happy. And if E-Before-I-Except-After-Y makes him happy, I'm all for it."

"Don't tell me that's what you used to call her when she was your teacher," said Ten.

"Yeah," Lana admitted. "All of us did. You know, that rule has plenty of exceptions."

When they got onto Lombard Street, she saw the Victorian where she lived and the first thing she noticed was the local ABC affiliate's news van parked out front.

"How did they know I was back?" she groaned.

"I should have checked before bringing you here," Ten said. "More than likely someone's been camped here since we brought Jeremy back to stand trial. He's been all over the news and I'm sure they want to hear your side of the story."

"Why can't they leave me alone?" Lana complained. "I don't want to talk to them."

Ten had slowed the SUV. Now he sped up. "No problem," he said. "You can stay with me for a few days."

Lana looked at him in surprise. "You wouldn't mind? It's not as if you've had time to prepare for a guest."

"My momma didn't raise a helpless slob, you know. I cook, clean *and* do windows."

Lana had to admit, twenty minutes later as she crossed his apartment's threshold, he hadn't been ex-aggerating. The pine floors gleamed, the walls were painted off-white, kind of unimaginative in her expert opinion, but pristine and it went well with the floors throughout the two-bedroom, two-thousand-square-foot space. In the living room he had masculine brown leather matching couches facing each other and a large square coffee table made of stressed wood sitting be-tween them. There was a fireplace in the living room with a mantel that gave the room a homey feel, and his bookshelves, which lined two walls, were filled with hardcover books. He really was a reader.

The kitchen was modern and fitted with stainless-steel appliances. She could tell he liked to cook. The placement of his island and cabinets were all for his convenience. He even had a long shock-absorbing mat in front of the sink and stove that offered relief from back pain should he be standing a long time at the work stations. "Your kitchen is very efficient," she said.

"I know," he said regrettably. "It's a bit sterile. But now that I've brought an interior decorator home I'm hoping she'll give me a few tips to liven it up."

"Color," was Lana's reply to that. "A deep, masculine brick red or maybe a forest green. But I like it. You've got good taste."

Ten was peering in the refrigerator. "Are you thirsty?"

"Yes," she said. She usually was after a long flight.

He handed her a bottle of spring water and took one for himself. Lana had left her bags in the living room by the door. She stood now wearing her favorite yellow sundress and a pair of macramé espadrilles, her legs and arms appeared even more golden-brown than before. Her shiny hair was in its natural curly state and it perfectly framed her face.

To Ten, she looked even more beautiful than he'd remembered her. Her warm brown eyes were looking deeply into his. She set her water bottle on the island and moved in. He casually backed against one of the tall stools around the island and set his bottle down, too. He sat atop the stool he'd backed into. Lana walked between his legs, and his arms enveloped her. Foreheads touched. Mouths met in tentative kisses. Little things that enticed, tested the limits of their patience, but were not really satisfying because both of them knew they were not going to be entirely happy until they were lying naked in each other's arms. But this was nice, too.

He inhaled her essence, his nostrils flaring. Her scent was heady. Like the initial effects of a drug. The good part, before you come crashing down.

"A bath would be relaxing," she murmured against his mouth.

Ten, already hardening, grew harder at the thought of seeing her naked. He took her by the hand. "Right this way."

He took her to his en suite bathroom, past the king-size bed, which she noticed was neatly made. The shower was huge and glass enclosed, and could easily accommodate two people. "No bathtub, huh?" she asked, looking around them.

"The other bathroom has a bathtub," he said. "Would you prefer a bath?"

"Is it big enough for two?"

"Nah," he said regrettably. "We're too tall to fit in it comfortably."

"Then the shower's good," she said, and began unbuttoning his shirt. This done, she ran her hands over his chest, relishing the feel of taut muscles and warm skin against her palms. She sensually tweaked his nipples between eager fingers. Peering into his eyes, she said, "I want to know everything that gives you pleasure."

"You're doing pretty well without my help," he said,

his desire mounting with every passing second. He ran his hand up her thigh. Under the sundress she was wearing a very brief pair of panties. He slipped his hand in front, inside the waistband, and Lana trembled with anticipation. He found her sweet spot and Lana moistened in an instant. He massaged her clitoris. Lana spread her legs wider. The man meant business. He was gentle but insistent. She grew wetter, his finger delved a little deeper, but maintained its lovely pressure. "Your pleasure gives me pleasure," he whispered as he bent and kissed her. His tongue claimed hers, manipulated it for her maximum enjoyment. She sighed and fell into him, opened herself to him. As the intensity increased in her feminine center, he could feel her release coming. He backed off, and let her feel as though pleasure was to be denied her. She tensed. Then he redoubled his efforts and brought her home. She called for him, her voice hoarse with satisfaction. For a moment, she closed her eyes. Opening them again, she looked him straight in the eye. "I'm a lucky girl."

"You're about to get luckier," he said, pulling her dress over her head. Her bra was next. Then her panties, which had earlier only been moved aside while he had his way with her. Now she stood before him in only the high-heeled espadrilles. He knelt and removed the shoes, making her feel like a princess whose prince had first taken every stitch of clothing off her body before letting her try on the glass slipper.

While still on his knees, he kissed her belly then rose to begin removing his own clothes and shoes.

Lana pressed her body close to his. His hard penis throbbed against her belly. She grabbed handfuls of his ass, which only made him more erect. Then he picked her up and carried her to the bed. They'd have to skip the shower for the time being.

He rummaged in the nightstand drawer and withdrew a latex condom, which he quickly rolled onto his member. He was so ready to take her he could barely stand it.

Lana shamelessly spread her legs, welcoming him inside of her. "Lana, Lana," he breathed as he entered her. She was speechless. She continued to ride the rising tide of their pleasure, her body in tune with his. Each thrust felt like it was rendering her asunder. She welcomed it. She wanted to be brought to the precipice and then forced over it. Not safe in his arms, but in peril of totally losing it.

She clung to him, her legs wrapped around him. Deeper and deeper Ten went, plunging with slow, sweet deliberation. He felt the muscles of her sex clenching around him. Holding him tightly, increasing his enjoyment to the point that all he wanted to do was to come and shout. But he wasn't going to come until he felt her convulsing beneath him again. Until her eyes took on that sleepy, dreamy aspect that told him she was fully satisfied.

She was panting softly, her legs loose and relaxed,

not as tightly wound around him as before. She pushed against him, arching her back. He felt the muscles of her sex clench and unclench repeatedly. Then he knew she'd climaxed. She continued to push against him as if offering herself up to him. His thrusts had become deeper and more rapid.

The orgasm claimed him. Perspiration dripped off his brow onto her chest. She held him in her arms. They convulsed together.

She finally spoke. "I planned on seducing you in the shower."

He got up and pulled her to her feet. Sweeping her into his arms, he said, "The shower it is."

Laughing, Lana wrapped her arms around his neck and held on. Life was definitely not going to be boring with Tennison Isles.

In the shower they lathered each other's bodies and took turns rinsing the soap off with the removable shower nozzle. "This is a great invention," Lana joked at one point. "I'm sure the inventor never thought people would be having sex with it when he dreamed it up."

A few minutes after they had gotten out of the shower, Ten was hard again. They'd gotten to his apartment around four that afternoon and they stayed in bed making love and talking until half past eight. After which their hunger pangs made them get up to go to the kitchen in search of food.

Ten made cheese omelets and toast, which they'd

eaten in bed while they watched the Turner Classic Movies channel. *The Learning Tree,* Gordon Parks's iconic film, had just gone off, and the closing credits were running.

"The way the characters were written seemed unrealistic," Lana said.

"True, the characters were kind of stereotypical," Ten agreed. "But you also have a white law-enforcement officer who was depicted as a racist. That was brave on Gordon Parks's part. I'm surprised the movie even got made back then."

Smiling at him, Lana said, "You *would* notice the cop."

They were sitting in bed cross-legged. She was wearing one of his big T-shirts whose hem fell to mid-thigh on her and he was in pajama bottoms. "Can't help it, it's in my blood," said Ten.

"You never wanted to be anything else?" she asked, stretching her legs out and reclining against the headboard.

"Oh, sure I did. When I was a kid I wanted to be the Black Panther."

"A black panther?" asked Lana, smiling. "You mean one of those radical black activists from the sixties?"

Ten laughed. "No, baby, *the* Black Panther, T'Challa," he said enthusiastically. "He was a superhero. His origin was African. He was a prince who defended his people. His family ruled the kingdom of Wakanda for centuries. He was cool. He was also badass."

"Are you talking about a comic-book superhero?"

"Yes, you mean you've never heard of him?"

"Was he a Marvel superhero like Captain America, Iron Man and The Hulk?"

"He's Marvel, yeah, but of course not nearly as well-known as those dudes. Obviously, since you've never heard of him."

"Why isn't he in those movies they're putting out every few months?"

"It's a conspiracy," Ten accused the Hollywood movie machine.

Lana was thoroughly enjoying this. Her man was a comic-book geek. She delighted in learning new things about him. "It is," she said of his conspiracy theory. "Couldn't Hollywood pump out at least one movie about a black superhero? I'm going to write somebody as soon as I get out of this bed!"

Laughing, Ten pulled her to him and wrapped her in his arms. "That won't be for a while." He kissed her and Lana forgot all about the Black Panther.

Chapter 13

Lana went back to her apartment on Monday. Ten dropped her off before reporting to work. It was very early and there were no news vans parked outside the Victorian. When she got inside, the first thing she did was open windows to air out the one-room apartment.

Although only about eight hundred square feet in size the apartment felt spacious because she kept clutter to a minimum and used furnishings that were classically styled. The colors on the walls gave the room the illusion of space. After opening all of the windows, she switched on the TV set mounted on the wall above the fireplace's mantel.

The weatherman said it would be in the lower eighties today. Not bad for late August.

Then, to her surprise, a rebroadcast of an interview
with Jeremy was aired. The very reporter whom she'd
spoken with a few weeks ago, Gary Randall, was sitting across from Jeremy in what was probably a common room in the county jail. Looking very pleased to
be speaking exclusively with Jeremy, Gary Randall
asked him how he was faring.

Jeremy, ever the opportunist, smiled into the camera. "They're treating me well, Gary. I can't complain."

Indeed, he looked in the peak of health. He had
blond roots, his hair having grown out since she last
saw him. And his skin appeared tanned and healthy.
She'd expected him to look sallow but he must be allowed time out in the sunshine to have maintained
his tan.

"That's not all true, is it, Mr. Corday?" Gary asked
with a smug look. "You've been complaining that your
wife, I'm sorry, your *ex-wife*, hasn't come to see you
since you've been incarcerated."

"I'm sure she has better things to do with her time,"
Jeremy said humbly. "I haven't exactly been the best
husband to her. Once I was in here I was given access
to old newspapers and I've read how the media went
after her while I was on the run. Yes, I admit it, I ran."
His expression was contrite. Lana sniffed derisively.
All they needed now was for a priest to come in there
and absolve him of all his sins. He looked like an innocent choirboy. "I know I have no right to ask anyone
for anything, but I'm asking the public to stop blam-

ing her for something I did. She didn't know what I was up to. She's totally innocent. If she's watching, I want her to know I'm sorry for conning her along with everybody else."

Okay, now she was not only surprised, but shocked. Why was he being magnanimous? What did he want from her?

"I think she's been justified," was Gary Randall's considered opinion. "I went to Kitty Hawk, North Carolina, recently to speak to several people who were in the bank the day you were captured. They say she played a pivotal role in your being brought to justice.

"Do you feel betrayed by her?"

Jeremy looked at Gary Randall as if the reporter should be ashamed of himself to suggest such a thing. "She did the right thing," Jeremy said, the sincerity pouring off him in waves. "I have no conscience. Lana was my conscience. She was my weakness, too. I never would have gone to the bank that day if I hadn't put my complete trust in her. The FBI lucked out when they recruited her."

"Like King Kong, you were brought down by a beauty," Gary observed.

"You loser," Lana said under her breath.

"I suppose you could say that," Jeremy said, briefly looking away from the camera to give the reporter a pointed glance, "If you want to sound like an idiot."

Gary cleared his throat. "You say you have no conscience. Are you disappointed you got caught?"

Jeremy laughed. "Of course I'm disappointed I got caught. I'd rather be spending that 250 million on some Caribbean island. I'm a con man. But I'm also realistic. I'm guilty and I'm going to pay for my crimes. So be it. Am I going to apologize to the people I cheated? No. I promised them easy money, and they got taken. I feel a little bad for the retirees I conned but most of my clients were rich bastards who deserved what they got."

"If you feel that way," asked Gary, "why should the public want to do you a favor and lay off your ex-wife?"

"Because they aren't without a conscience like I am," said Jeremy reasonably. He rose and called for the guard.

Gary Randall smiled for the camera. "I guess our interview is over."

Lana switched off the TV.

Less than a minute later, her phone rang. It was Ten. "Pete just phoned me and told me Jeremy's on TV right now."

"I saw it," Lana told him. "I don't know what to make of it, but I saw it."

She gave Ten the gist of the interview. "He's got nothing to gain from what he did" was his opinion. "Maybe he really is sorry for the way he treated you and is attempting to atone for it."

"It's nice you can give him the benefit of the doubt," Lana said. "But I'm not ready to do that."

"I'm not trying to rush you through the process,"

Ten said. "I have a meeting in a few minutes. Talk to you later, sweetheart."

Lana smiled. "All right, see you tonight."

Shortly after she hung up, the phone rang again. This time it was Gia. "Gia," she cried, happy to hear from her friend. "How are you?"

"I'm so glad you're back," Gia told her. "How're you? You sound good."

"I am good," Lana told her.

Gia rushed on, "My in-laws were here all July and they loved the house. What's more, I recommended you to several of my San Francisco friends. Have you listened to your messages?"

Lana perked up. "No, I haven't gotten around to doing that."

"Then get to it, girlfriend," cried Gia. "Let's go to lunch soon."

Lana said goodbye, and checked the display on the answering machine. There were fourteen messages. She immediately pressed the play button.

The first message was from Grant. "Lana, why didn't you tell me you were in the Outer Banks helping the FBI nab Jeremy?" He laughed. "Was that story about your father being sick true? Call me."

The rest of the messages were either from people who wanted to hire her, or people who wanted to rehire her. She got some satisfaction out of hearing from people who had dropped her without waiting to learn if she were innocent or guilty. Now they were saying things like "I never believed a word they said about you."

A woman who had been hiring Lana for the past six years to redecorate her house with each season change cooed, "Darling, call me. I'm at the mercy of a decorator from hell! I need you desperately."

The same woman that had stopped taking her calls eight months ago.

Lana decided she would call her, but not today.

She listened to the rest of the messages. Every one of them was positive and rich with possibilities. And this had happened prior to Jeremy's so-called plea for the public to give her a break. Maybe her business would survive, after all.

For the next few weeks, Lana got back into her work routine. She enjoyed nothing more than accepting the challenge of transforming a room into a place that not only reflected the taste of those who resided in it but was functional and beautiful. She often worked late, but she and Ten made the time to see each other in the evenings when he was in town. He had been told that he was being considered for the position of special-agent-in-charge of the San Francisco office, however in the meantime he and his team were on the trail of a killer, Augustine Rush. Rush was a physicist at the University of California. He'd learned his wife was cheating on him and snapped, killing her lover, a colleague of his at the university. Lana was again reminded of the fact that snap decisions often ruined your life. He had been a respected member of academia. Now he was a fugitive.

That night, Ten had phoned her and told her he was on the way to an address right in the city because Rush had been spotted there.

"Be careful. I love you," she told him.

"I love you," he'd murmured with sweet intensity and hung up.

She'd gone back to the drafting table in the corner of her apartment where she made sketches of ideas she had for rooms she was designing. A cup of coffee sat to the side and she had music playing low.

Meanwhile, across town, at the San Remo Hotel on Mason Street, Ten, Pete, Carrie and Eduardo were deciding how best to enter the building. Ten had Carrie and Eduardo go around back in case Rush tried to flee via the fire escape. The hotel was a renovated Italianate originally constructed in 1906. The rooms were built around an atrium.

There was no need to go inside the hotel to get to Rush's room. The outside stairs gave them access. Ten and Pete scaled the stairs and Ten knocked on Rush's room door. "Augustine Rush, this is the FBI, open the door!"

There was silence for a full thirty seconds, then a tremulous voice from within proclaimed, "You have the wrong room, there is no Augustine Rush here!"

Pete whispered, "He's not gonna try that, is he?"

"Then open the door and show us some ID to that effect, and we'll gladly leave you alone," said Ten. His gun was already drawn. Rush had killed his colleague with a handgun. He could very well still have it on him.

"Wait a minute," said the voice. "I have to put on some clothes."

Inside the room, Augustine Rush, a slight, dark-haired, middle-aged man who always looked in need of a shave, tried to pry open the window, but it hadn't been opened in such a long time it was difficult to do so, plus it squeaked loudly. Try as he might, the window wouldn't open sufficiently enough to climb out of it. So in a panic, he threw a chair through it.

Ten and Pete heard the clear sound of the impact of the chair hitting the window and the breaking glass. Ten kicked the door in. Pete went in low and was greeted with Rush's back end as the physicist scampered through the opening where the window had been. Pete went after him. Ten went after Pete.

Rush didn't get far. Carrie and Eduardo were on the landing just below the fire escape waiting for him. He saw them as he was climbing down, and began climbing back up. He had a handgun wedged in his waistband. He took it out and pointed it at Pete. His hand was shaking so badly, Pete thought it best to freeze. Ten's feet had just hit the steel of the fire escape when Rush cried, "I'm not going to prison. I'd die in there. I'd rather die here." And he put the gun to his right temple and tried to pull the trigger.

Ten couldn't believe it. Another instance of the safety still being on.

Rush figured it out quickly, though. He flicked the release with his thumb and tried again. By that time, Pete had grabbed his gun hand, pointed the weapon toward the night sky, and delivered a punch to the physicist's soft belly. Rush struggled with the strength of a desperate man. Suddenly the gun went off and the round caught Ten in the left shoulder. The sound of the report must have sobered Rush because he abruptly stopped fighting Pete, who got the gun out of his grasp and knocked the physicist onto the ground.

"Scientists," muttered Ten, clutching his shoulder. "They're more dangerous than bank robbers."

Pete called down to Carrie and Eduardo, "Get an ambulance, Ten's been shot."

Ten's been shot. Those three words struck terror in Lana's heart when, a few minutes later, Pete phoned her with the news.

Lana made record time getting to San Francisco General. When she got there, Pete was waiting for her out front as he'd said he would be. He escorted her upstairs to the operating room's waiting area where Carrie and Eduardo already were.

Carrie came to her and hugged her. "Hey, girl, get that panicked look off your face, he's going to be okay."

After Carrie let her go Lana forced a smile for the tall blonde, breathed in and let it out in a long exhale. "Logically I knew this day might come, but I still wasn't prepared for how nerve-racking it is realizing Ten could have been killed."

"I know," said Carrie sympathetically. She led Lana over to the couch where she had been sitting with Eduardo. Lana said hello to Eduardo, who gave her a smile and reached for her hand. She gave it to him and he squeezed it reassuringly. "It's just a shoulder wound. Ten has been through worse."

Her mind went back to that inch-long raised scar on his side just above his waist. He hadn't volunteered any information about it, and she hadn't asked, but she'd certainly noticed it. "You mean that scar he has?"

Eduardo's dark eyes met hers. "He didn't tell you how he got it?"

Lana shook her head. "I'm getting the feeling he wants to protect me from the violent side of his job."

"Well, maybe I shouldn't tell you," said Eduardo out of loyalty to Ten.

Lana glared at him. "Tell me, Eduardo!"

Eduardo looked to Carrie for support, but Carrie just shrugged. "It'll keep her mind occupied while we're waiting to hear how the surgery went."

Eduardo sighed. "Okay, so seven years ago, we— Ten and I, this was before Pete and Carrie joined the team—were investigating a kidnapping. A man in his twenties had snatched a seventeen-year-old from her high school's grounds. She'd been communicating with him online. Thought it was harmless fun. He became obsessed with her. She made the mistake of giving him details about her life. She thought she was being safe by not actually giving him her name and address. But she told him which school she attended and was naive enough to send him a recent photo."

Lana was watching Eduardo intently, hanging on his every word. Ten had told her stories about some of his cases but he hadn't mentioned this one.

"One afternoon, as soon as school was out, he was waiting on the curb in a van that he'd equipped with restraints. I'm sure he'd gone over it in his mind many times—snatch the girl, kicking and screaming. It didn't matter because he was a big guy and could easily handle her. He wasn't concerned about some student coming to her rescue because people are basically afraid of crazies. They try to avoid being a victim themselves so they generally give them a wide berth. And it unfolded exactly as he envisioned it. He grabbed her from in the midst of several hundred students eager to get home from school, threw her in the van, locked her in the shackles, which he'd bolted to the floor of the van, and sped off."

"Oh, my God," said Lana amazed by the man's boldness.

"He was single-minded," Eduardo commented. "Jacob Lee Caan."

When he said the name, Lana remembered. Jacob Lee Caan was now serving a life sentence in prison. The girl he'd kidnapped, Amy Roberts, had been rescued three days after he'd taken her. One of the agents had been stabbed by Caan during the rescue and had nearly died from the wound.

She'd seen a report on TV but the name of the agent had escaped her memory as soon as she'd finished watching it. Or perhaps Ten's name had never been mentioned.

The FBI liked a certain amount of anonymity.

She let Eduardo finish telling the story because she wanted to hear the details.

"Where did he take her?" she asked softly.

"Now, there, his preparation for the crime was flawed," Eduardo said with a smile. "This being his first kidnapping, he didn't realize that to keep someone against their will for any length of time required a place where you could be sure she wouldn't be heard or seen by nosy neighbors. Caan lived in a neighborhood that had seen better days but there were still good honest people there. Such a family lived next door. The mother of the family had always been wary of him. Anyway, while he was away from the house the woman next door heard a banging on Caan's basement window. Their kitchen window faced his basement window. Somehow the victim, Amy Roberts, had gotten loose but couldn't get out of the door, which was securely bolted. So she started banging on the basement window with everything she had. The neighbor woman ran over there and saw the poor girl and ran back home to phone the police. Unfortunately, she didn't make it because Caan returned just in time to see her running away from the window, caught her and knocked her out and dragged her downstairs to his basement, too. Now he had two hostages."

Lana's face filled with horror.

"But by that time, from eyewitness descriptions of Caan and his van, we'd narrowed it down to two persons—him and some other guy who'd recently been released from prison and had an MO quite similar to how Caan had snatched Amy Roberts. One team was checking out the other guy's address. Ten and I were checking out Caan's. Apparently we got there a couple hours after he'd thrown the neighbor in with Amy Roberts. He pretended to be cooperating with us, answered all our questions, even offered us refreshments. Before answering the door, he'd taken the time to gag and tie up the two females in his basement."

"Well, how did you suspect he was the guy?" Lana was anxious to know.

Eduardo smiled slowly. "Ten is very observant. While we were standing in the living room, he noticed a woman's shoe lying under a table. He casually asked Caan if the woman of the house was at home. Caan, who was sweating by now, said he lived alone. 'Then whose shoe is that?' Ten asked. Caan took on the appearance of a cornered rat and tried to run. He got as far as the kitchen before Ten grabbed him. When he turned around Ten saw a butcher's knife in his hand, but it was too late, Caan rammed the knife into his side.

I rounded the corner and put a bullet in Caan's shoulder right about the spot where Ten got shot tonight. I cuffed him, and then called for backup. The women were freed, but Ten spent hours in the operating room because the blade had punctured his lung."

"That must have taken a while to heal," Lana said. And she'd tried to run him to death. She felt bad for that stunt all over again.

"It took months for him to get a clean bill of health from his doctor, but he came back strong as ever. You know him, he's in great shape," Eduardo told her.

Ten's doctor came into the waiting room and all four of them got to their feet. She wore her natural hair in dreadlocks and had a pair of black-framed glasses perched on her nose. "Are you the family of Tennison Isles?" she asked.

Lana stepped forward. "Ten doesn't have any family in town. I'm his girlfriend and these are his friends."

The doctor held out her hand, "Hello." She smiled at Lana. "I'm Dr. Katharine Samuels. Tennison came through the operation with no complications. He's expected to make a full recovery. Right now he's waking up, and you should be able to see him in a few minutes. I'll send a nurse out to get you."

Lana had listened without interrupting. She pumped the doctor's hand. "Thank you, Dr. Samuels. Thank you so much!"

Katharine Samuels smiled again and said, "Just doing my job. You folks take care."

And she was gone.

The team was all smiles when Lana turned back around to face them.

"I told you he'd be fine," Carrie said.

"He's the man of steel," Pete quipped.

"Solid as a rock," Eduardo agreed.

After a beat, Eduardo said, "Well, we're going to head out, Lana. Tell Ten we'll drop in and check on him tomorrow and to get some rest."

Carrie hugged her briefly. "Just giving you some private time," she said for Lana's ears only. Lana suspected she was explaining their behavior because she was a newbie to their circle. She was grateful for their thoughtfulness. She didn't want to burst out crying in front of them and, the way she felt right now, emotional and relieved that Ten had pulled through the operation, she just might turn on the waterworks.

Sure, Eduardo had assured her a shoulder wound was nothing compared to other injuries Ten had endured. But what did Eduardo know? People had gone into the operating room and not been able to be revived from the anesthesia. Any number of disasters could have occurred.

After the agents had gone, leaving her alone in the waiting room, she raised her eyes heavenward, and said, "Thank You, God."

Ten smiled at her when she walked into the recovery room. They'd bandaged him and put him in a green hospital gown. Being such a big man he looked out of place in that small bed. The moment she saw his face, she started crying.

"Do I look that bad?" he asked, still smiling.

Lana went to him and grasped his hand in hers. She was afraid to hug him for fear she'd hurt him. But she placed his hand on her cheek, and then she turned her face and kissed his palm. "No, you look wonderful, gorgeous and alive!"

Ten chuckled. "Yes, I'm alive, my love, and I plan to stay that way for a long time."

A nurse bustled in and said, "I'm sorry, miss, but Mr. Isles needs to get some rest now. You can come back tomorrow during regular visiting hours."

Disappointed, Lana cried, "Visiting hours are over?"

"I'm afraid so," said the nurse nicely but firmly.

Lana clung to Ten's hand. "I'll be here first thing in the morning."

"I'm not going anywhere," said Ten.

Lana reluctantly let go of his hand. She bent and kissed his forehead.

"Oh, no," Ten protested, "the forehead kiss this early in our relationship. Are things going downhill already?"

Lana smiled and gently kissed his lips. "Better?"

Dimples showed in his cheeks. "Much better, thank you."

Chapter 14

Ten was advised by Dr. Samuels to stay home from work for at least four weeks. But after he returned to work, he would still have to avoid heavy lifting for another two months before his shoulder would be fully healed.

Lana enjoyed spoiling him and practically moved into his apartment while he was recovering. She had been there waiting for him when he'd gotten home from the hospital. As they lounged lazily intertwined on the couch, the doorbell rang at around two in the afternoon.

"Are you expecting anyone?" Lana asked as she rose to go see who was there.

"No," said Ten, puzzled. "I haven't even ordered anything recently."

Lana went to the side window and moved the curtain aside. From that angle she could see an elderly couple standing on the portico, suitcases at their sides.

"Do Jehovah's Witnesses carry huge suitcases around with them?" she asked Ten.

The African-American couple both had gray hair. The woman was a foot shorter than the man, and both seemed fit and healthy and were dressed casually.

"Open the door and see, sweetheart," said Ten from the couch.

Lana opened the door, a warm smile on her face. "Hello," she said, "how can I help you?"

The woman laughed. "Are you Lana?" she asked, her brown eyes twinkling with merriment. Those eyes—Lana recognized them anywhere. They were Ten's eyes.

Lana swung the door open wider. "Yes," she answered the woman. "I'm Lana, and you're Mrs. Isles, aren't you?"

Ten heard this and immediately tried to get up without disturbing his wound. Dr. Samuels had said any sudden movements might make the stitches come apart. The pain was immediate so he thought it best to behave himself and he sat back down.

"Mom?" he called.

"Yes, I am," Portia Isles answered Lana, a grin on her face. "And this is Ten's father, Ben." Lana loved her Southern-accented voice.

Benjamin Isles inclined his curly head in Lana's

direction, "A pleasure, Lana." He was nearly as tall as his son and his skin color was close to Ten's as well, a deep golden-brown, whereas his wife had dark-chocolate skin that looked smooth, silky and extremely youthful for a woman in her seventies. Ten had told her his mother was seventy-three and his father was seventy-eight.

"Come in, come in," Lana cried, embarrassed that she'd been frozen in her tracks for a few moments. But it wasn't every day your boyfriend's parents showed up out of the blue. She went to grab one of the suitcases but Ben told her, "I've got those." And he picked them up as though they weighed next to nothing.

Portia went straight to her baby boy on the couch. Ben stepped into the foyer, put down the suitcases and then followed Lana into the living room.

By the time the two of them entered the room, Portia was fluffing up the pillows behind Ten's back. "Mom, Dad, why didn't you tell me you were coming? I would've had you picked up at the airport."

"That's why," Portia said as she moved around the couch, and sat down beside her son. "We didn't want to put you to any trouble. You already went and got yourself shot!"

"It wasn't as if I invited the perp to take a potshot at me," Ten said with a laugh. "Tell her, Dad."

His father sat down on an accent chair across from his son and his wife. Lana went and perched on the arm of the sofa on the opposite side of Ten so that he was now flanked by his mother and Lana.

"Now, Portia," Ben said soothingly to his wife, "you've been here less than five minutes. Give the boy a break."

"Anyway," Portia said, pointedly not offering up an apology for her opinion, "when are you going to introduce us to Lana?"

Ten laughed again. "I distinctly heard you introduce yourself to her a minute ago," he said, "but as a formal introduction—Lana, please meet my parents, Portia and Benjamin Isles of Danville, Virginia. Mom and Dad, this is Lana Braithwaite-Corday."

"I'm pleased to meet you both," Lana said, smiling at Portia and Ben. "Ten has told me so many wonderful things about you."

"Such as?" Portia asked, eyeing Lana with amusement.

"Mom, behave," Ten told her sternly. "Lana, my mother has a habit of mercilessly teasing people she likes and she obviously took one look at you and decided she likes you. So feel free to give as good as you get from her. Otherwise she'll think she intimidates you."

Portia harrumphed. "Giving my secrets away already. He must really like you, Lana."

Lana smiled. "I'm glad because I really like him," she said. She could tell that she was going to have to stay alert around Portia Isles.

Ten cleared his throat. "Mom, Dad, you've been here before. You know where the guest room is—make yourselves at home. Are you hungry? Want a drink?"

Ben spoke up, "No, son, we're fine. I, for one, could use a little nap after that plane ride, though. Come on, Portia. Put your man to bed."

In their absence Lana said, "But they just got here."

Ten laughed softly. "Sweetie, that's just Dad's way of getting Mom alone so he can reprimand her in private. I've never known those two to argue in front of anyone. There was something she did that got his goat, as he used to describe anyone making him angry, and he wants to discuss it with her. My mom is the talkative one, outgoing and often the center of attention. My dad's quiet, reflective and incapable of raising his voice. They're total opposites."

"But opposites attract," Lana finished for him.

"Exactly," said Ten. He patted the couch's cushion on his right side, and Lana moved to sit closer.

"Listen, sweetie, my mother is here for one reason and one reason alone, to check you out."

"But you got shot in the line of duty," Lana said, believing that was the reason his parents had shown up. To reassure themselves their son was all right.

"No, they knew I was in no danger of dying from a shoulder wound. My dad was a policeman for thirty years after he got out of the army. He's been shot before. I'm just warning you so you'll know. Portia Isles is cagey."

"A woman acquires certain skills after parenting ten kids," Lana said knowingly.

"Lana, that meal was delicious," Portia said a few evenings later after dinner while she and Lana cleaned the kitchen. "Where'd you learn to cook? Ten told me you lost your mother when you were eight."

"My dad taught me," Lana said, smiling at the thought of her first cooking lesson—pancakes. "He learned from his mom and dad who were both great cooks."

"Ah, yes, I've read your father's books. How is he?"

"He's great, he recently told me he's in love and is going to get married after being a widower for nearly twenty-five years."

"Now that's something," Portia exclaimed. "What's she like, the woman he fell in love with?"

Lana laughed shortly. "She's kind and loves people. She was my high school English teacher. I was wary in the beginning, but she won me over."

"Because you love your father and you think she's good for him," Portia rightly guessed.

Lana nodded. "Yes. He's been alone a lot of years. He was so devoted to my mother, but he deserves happiness, especially in his golden years. With Ellen there with him, I won't have to worry about him as much."

"But you never stop worrying about the people you love," Portia told her sagely.

"I, for example, worry about each of my children.

Whether they're making the right choices in life, their health, and everything else my mind can come up with to worry about.

"Sometimes I wish I could turn off the worry switch and simply be content that no matter what they do, it's meant to be and I can't control it, anyway, so why worry?"

"Yet, you worry," Lana said, smiling at her.

Portia sighed, and hung the dish towel she'd been using to dry the dishes over the bar on the door of the oven. Lana noticed that wasn't where Ten put his dish towels to dry. There was a bar on the inside of the cabinet door under the sink. She was really starting to pay attention to his habits.

"Yes, I worry too much about them. Even though, they don't want me worrying about them and warn that it only raises my blood pressure."

"They don't understand that you thrive on worrying about them," Lana said, shocking Portia.

Portia smiled at her with a look of awe in her dark eyes. "Is that sick, or what?"

"No, it's not sick," Lana denied. "It's a habit you've practiced for so long, it's as effortless as breathing. But, sick? I don't think so."

"It *is* a sick practice when I traveled all the way from Danville just to stick my nose where it doesn't belong. My husband didn't want to come, but he wouldn't let me travel all this way on my own, either. So that's why he's here, too."

"Has Ten told you that he loves me?" Lana asked curiously.

"Of course, he did," Portia confirmed, "and that scared the hell out of me. Ten's never said that about any other woman. I had to meet you. But I told myself if I liked you upon first sight, I was going to go with the feeling and not try to dislike you simply because it appears that due to your background you're not suitable for Ten."

That hurt. In spite of Lana having no expectation of being liked by Ten's parents it hurt that his mother had already formed an opinion of her character without having met her. "You mean because of my former marriage."

Portia looked genuinely regretful. "Yes, Lana, and it's not because your ex-husband turned out to be a con artist. It's because of how your marriage might have affected you. Will your heart harden and not be able to love, really love, someone else because of how you were treated by your first husband?" She sighed. "I know a little about recovering from a betrayal. I was not an innocent little virgin when I married Ben. I'd been married before. To a man who would go off and stay away for weeks, chasing other women, then come home to me and expect everything to be as he left it. After I got rid of him, it took me a while to allow Ben—who was perfect for me, but I couldn't see it— into my hard, hard heart." She grinned suddenly. "I admit I went a little overboard with the kids after learning I could love Ben. After the eighth pregnancy, Ten's birth, I told Ben, 'You've got to nip it in the bud!'"

It took Lana a beat or two to figure out to what Portia was referring.

"Oh, you mean he got a vasectomy!"

"Yes, dear, he had to nip that thing in the bud," Portia confirmed.

Lana looked Portia in the eyes. She really liked this woman. She was the type of woman she imagined her mother was, honest and unafraid to tell it like it was. "It seems you've made a trip for nothing," she said softly, and smiled with tears in her eyes. "Because I love Ten. I love him with my whole heart. Not holding anything back because I've had enough falsehood in my life. I want the unadulterated truth now. And I know I'll get it from Ten. I love him and I know I'll always love him, through good times and bad times. I'm tougher than I look, Mrs. Isles."

Portia Isles had tears in her eyes, too. She held her arms open and hugged Lana. "That's good because life can be tough. We women have to be tougher than life to get through it with our sense of humor intact."

The next day Lana was sad to see Portia and Ben depart for the airport, once again declaring their independence by not allowing her to drive them.

She and Ten stood in the doorway of his apartment, waving goodbye. Momentarily, Ten shut the door and they went back inside. "They love you," he said with confidence.

"I love them, too," she said truthfully.

"Then you wouldn't mind having them for in-laws?" asked Ten, watching her so intently that Lana felt naked under his scrutiny, vulnerable and completely taken aback by his question. "In-laws?" she asked dumbly.

"That's what they'd be if you married me," he said reasonably.

"Are you sure you want to marry a woman who quite possibly can't have children?" she asked, nervously. "I'm thirty-two. Maybe my eggs have dried up by now. You'd be the shame of the Isles family what with how virile the men are and how fertile the women are."

"I'll take my chances," Ten said with a smirk.

Laughing, Lana answered his question with a resounding, "Yes, yes, I'll marry you."

She was careful not to hurt his shoulder when she kissed him.

Epilogue

Six months later they were married at her father's house in the Outer Banks. They'd chosen that location because most of her friends were there, and Ten's family wouldn't have as long a trip since the majority of them lived in neighboring Virginia.

Ten became the special-agent-in-charge of the San Francisco office. Lana continued to work as an interior designer. And nearly a year after they were married they welcomed Tennison Jr. into the world.

Three years after they were wed they were visiting Aaron and Ellen at their house. Lana and her dad sat on the back deck observing Ten and two-year-old Ten Jr. playing Frisbee on the beach with Bowser. Ellen was inside working on her first novel. With encouragement from Aaron, she was turning her love of reading into a writing career just as he'd done many years ago.

It was a beautiful summer day. Lana looked out at her husband and son with a contented smile on her face. Her dad, though, frowned. "When are you going to cut that boy's hair? He looks like a girl."

Lana laughed. She'd let Ten Jr.'s hair, which was thick and curly like his father's, but reddish-brown like hers, grow down his back. She loved his hair. "He does not!" she disagreed. "And I don't want you saying that around him."

"I'd never do that," Aaron was quick to say. He smiled at the sight his grandson made. He was big for his age, and strong. He would probably one day surpass his father in height.

"What are you hoping for this time?" he asked his daughter who had a noticeable baby bump.

Lana put her hand over her belly. "I don't have to hope, I know we're having twins."

"Boys, or girls?" asked Aaron.

"Girls," Lana said.

"Ten and Ten and a half will be outnumbered by females," Aaron said. "Ten will want to try for another boy."

Lana sighed. "That's what I get for marrying a tenth son. And don't think I don't know you're just trying to wangle another grandchild out of me."

* * * * *

REQUEST YOUR FREE BOOKS!

2 FREE NOVELS
PLUS 2 FREE GIFTS!

KIMANI™
ROMANCE

Love's ultimate destination!

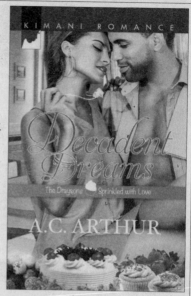

Undeniable passion that is forbidden…

Beneath Southern *Skies*

TERRA LITTLE

Gossip columnist Vanessa Valentino is forced to return back home after digging up one scandalous secret too many. Now she must face Nathaniel Woodberry—her sworn enemy! Yet Vanessa can't turn off her longing for the irresistible investigative journalist. And he can't help but seduce the former Southern belle with a healthy dose of down-home passion.

Join five of today's hottest romance authors

New York Times Bestselling Authors

LORI FOSTER
BRENDA JACKSON

USA TODAY Bestselling Authors

CATHERINE MANN * VIRNA DePAUL * JULES BENNETT

as they unleash the passionate thrills of new love
in one sizzling original collection

Available wherever books are sold!